The Beginning

Tara Moats

ISBN-13: 9798679574151

Cover design by: Art Painter
Library of Congress Control Number: 2018675309
Printed in the United States of America

To my loving wife Dania, my sister Amanda and my good friend Carol, thank you for believing in me. This has been a long time coming and I could never have finished without all of you.

Contents

Chapter one

What about Me?

As I stand here looking into the mirror, I feel so lonely today. I feel like I should be able to pick up the phone and call her. I feel like this has all been one bad dream that I cannot wake up from. I feel as though my whole world has shrunk into just my home that nothing else exists outside of the home. I am so alone now. The loneliness that settles in like a cold breeze chilling you to your very bones...

Last year I received a phone call from Bill (the husband of my best friend Cassie) that Cassie had been hit by a car while crossing the street on her way to meet Bill for lunch. One second, she is full of life and crossing the street the next she is being mowed down by a stolen car running from the police. It was all too much, how could this be? I felt responsible as I had a dream about this happening for months, waking up drenched in sweat and shaking at the thought of losing Cassie, telling myself it was just a dream, just a damn dream. I did not warn her, I just ignored it. I felt such guilt and shame. Her injuries were just as I had dreamed. Her spleen and her liver ruptured, multiple broken bones and severe head injury. She had died within minutes of impact. My only solace was that she did not have to suffer.

Suffering is more than anyone should have to endure. Like the suffering her husband and two small children still had to endure with her gone. I still see them, the kids and Bill. I take them to the park and out to eat when I can drag myself out to be around people which is getting harder and harder these days.

I feel a dread come over me, and then fear grip my heart. My breath catches in my throat and I am forced to stop at the door and go back inside my house, my hell and my sanctuary. I am not sure when it happened or how I became that way. I was not a complete shut-in, but pretty damn close. I know it is not just because of Cassie but here I am, barely able to leave my house at times due to the anxiety that fills me, a dread that paralyzes every part of me. I do not know how Bill and the kids are able to carry on. He gets up and goes to work every day, the kids to school. Most days he seems fine, other days when you look in his eyes you can tell that he has been crying, for hours from the look of him. I guess we all just have to continue on the end of our journey, with or without someone beside us.

Oh Cassie, how I miss you? We had been friends since middle school. She was my best friend and had been for years. Over the years we had shared everything that sisters would have shared, the birth of her kids, me coming out, and everything in between. Now she was gone, just a vault full of memories in my mind that made my heart ache every time I pulled a memory out. I missed everything about her, her dark hair and brown eyes, her dry humor and amazing wit. I missed the way she always knew when something was bothering me even though I would insist there was nothing wrong. She brought the sunshine into an otherwise dreary day, and I loved her so much, my friend. Your life was cut short way too soon. Stop! Stop this wallowing Cassie would have said, she never would have wanted this. Life is to be lived, she would have said, so go and live it. I have to keep reminding myself otherwise I would sink into the abyss of loss forever to be alone and lonely without human contact.

Looking back into the mirror, I can see the tears running down my face, as I wipe them away I think to myself; "when does it get easier?" I look down at the sink barely focusing and see a bottle of cologne, (I remember the smell like it was yesterday sporty and slightly musky) that I knew did not belong to me, it was hers, my ex. Great, now I get to change my focus from one disaster to another.

Drowning in my own misery, I allowed my mind to think about the last relationship I was in. I had allowed that misery to ruin a relationship that was already on shaky ground. Truth be told, it was just an excuse to be done with it. It has been a few months since I ended my last relationship and I was hoping it would get easier. Thinking back, I do not see what we ever saw in each other other than the sex. Why would I choose someone arrogant, judgmental, and egotistical? What does anyone ever see in another that sparks an attraction? A look, a smile, or a shared moment? To have nothing in common, but still find each other. Why is it that some people can make this connection work for years and others for only the briefest of moments? Thinking back over the past couple of years, I cannot see where we were destined for anything other than a breakup. I wanted so much to believe that we would make it. A hopeless romantic, that's me or at least it was. Was I looking for something that I wanted to exist, but that did not? I really hate these moments when my reflection on past events turns into moments of depression and sadness. Looking at my self in the mirror, I wondered to myself, "What is wrong with me?" "Anxiety, depression, and sadness?" A huge sigh escapes…

I am a well-educated woman. I have a master's degree behind me and continuing with graduate school, but to what end? I am not sure yet. Taking online classes has been challenging for someone who procrastinates with the simplest of tasks. My work is my haven, the place that centers me. I have allowed my work to take over most of my waking hours, between that and school reflection takes up only a small place in my world anymore. So how is it that days like this are still possible?

I am so tired. I am tired of being both alone and lonely. I am tired of trying to make a relationship work. Tired of balancing the give and take in a relationship with someone who only takes and hardly ever gives of herself. I am tired of this one-sided roller-coaster ride in which the other person takes what she needs, then moves on, and never looks back at the devastation left in her wake. I am just tired.

For the past several weeks, I have become something of a shut-in. If I do not go out, then I cannot get hurt, right? I do not want to be vulnerable to someone who can turn my world upside down again. On one hand, I long for the closeness and companionship of another loving soul. However, on the other hand, I want to save myself the misery of what is to come next: the end, be it the end of life or the end of a relationship, just the end.

Some would say I am too young to be feeling this way, but I feel as if my soul has been around for a long time. If I believed in reincarnation, I would say that I must have lived a dozen lives, each life more devoid of love than the last. Whatever lesson I was to have learned to progress into a better next life must have been lost on me, for I feel my torment is centuries old.

So here I am, looking at my image in the mirror, feeling wary and run down. In a few more days, I need to psych myself up for a trip back home. I do not necessarily like the trip itself but once I am there, it is generally a good thing. I have some good memories there with my family. Although they can be a little strange, they are my family, and they do love me. I am not always the nicest person. Sometimes I am damn hard to deal with; I can be arrogant, assertive (even aggressive should I feel the need to be), and even a little bossy. Nevertheless, to my family, blood is blood and for that, forgiveness is never far behind.

Enough of this, now it is time to get ready for work, and one of the few occasions that I must actually go into the office. I have grown accustomed to working from home and being able to set my own work hours. My boss is very flexible. As long as I log in the forty hours a week, she is good with it. We have a special computer program that logs my hours for me. I work generally more than forty hours a week, so my boss does not mind. Today is a special day; we are going nationwide with an online utilization review network. Until today, only a handful of hospitals were participants. Now, every hospital that is using computer charting can be reviewed online.

Unfortunately, everyone involved in the company is required to be at the kickoff of the "go-live national" campaign which includes me. I really do hate large crowds and this event promises to be a three-ring circus. I might just as well "bite the bullet" and get ready to go. I hate that drive into work. I hate it almost as much as having to actually be at work. As I climb into my car, my mind begins to wander. I find myself thinking of the past again, "just stop it, damn it!" I scream into the rearview mirror. At that moment, a Mercedes almost runs me off the road, "Watch where you're going dumb ass!" I screamed. Doesn't anyone know how to drive anymore? What the hell? I know the dumb ass did not hear me, but at least I feel better for having said it. It is a shame that you cannot go a mile without someone speeding, cutting you off, or almost running you over. I try to calm myself down by thinking of something else, my trip back home. It will be so nice to go back home. Things are so much slower there. People do not seem to be in as much of a hurry, I miss that. People there still do not know how to drive but most of them are the damn tourists anyway.

Well, here I am. I am so glad I have a parking space with my name on it. Otherwise, I would never find a place to park around here. Ok, once again time to "bite the bullet" and go inside, ugh.

"Corrine? Damn it, Corrine! I told you, NO, interviews prior to the "go-live" time." Mani yelled from across the room, as she looked into her office to find two well-dressed reporters waiting for an interview. Some things never change around here, I laughed to myself. Mani is always screeching at someone, but always with good cause (at least she thinks so).

"I know, they are just waiting in your office, boss. I told them, no interview until afterward." Corrine stated apologetically. "I wasn't sure where else to put them. I know you didn't want them in the conference room until you were sure all glitches were ironed out, right?" "Well duh, that didn't take a damn brain surgeon to figure that out. Now, get them out of my office, put them in the break room, or one of the small conference rooms.

"$*$^#@ %#&*%^......" Mani continued to rant for a few more minutes until the reporters were actually walking out of her office, then, with her best award-winning smile, ushered them through. "How lovely of you to join us today, it will be a while longer. However, Miss. Colone will be glad to get you whatever you need. Drinks? Food? A Bathroom, maybe?" Mani always knew how to break the ice. "Ms. Walden, if I may ask you one question?" the taller of the two reporters spoke up looking confused. "Of course," Mani said, shooting a dirty look at Corrine. "What time will the kickoff be, and how long do you anticipate before we can start our interview?" The taller man questioned. I could tell he caught Mani off guard. Rarely did anyone ever catch Mani off guard. "Well, that is two questions, but since you asked so nicely. The kickoff starts in 10 minutes and should take no longer than 30-45 minutes barring any unforeseen complications." Mani was back on her game and always quick to recover. I loved to watch her toy with her prey, and I could tell he would soon be her prey. I could not help laughing to myself for Mani would be well suited with this one; something about him told me she was going to have her hands full with this one.

What was that strange sensation I felt down my back? My Granny would have said, "Somebody just walked over your grave, child." That is what she would say if she was still alive. What does that mean anyway? How can someone walk over your grave if you are still alive?

I feel a strange coldness in the air chilling me to the very core of my being. What is causing me to feel this way? Something is not right. I cannot put my finger on it, but the feeling will not go away. For now, I will put it out of my mind. There is too much riding on this project. I have earned stock in this company and have a vested interest in its well-being, at this point, failure is not an option. I cannot shake the feeling that something big is going to happen. At least the feeling is not associated with work, but what?

"Ok, everyone let's get this party started." Jules always did have a way with words. "In another 10, 9, 8, 7...." As the countdown continued, I found it hard to keep my mind from wandering back to that weird feeling. However, now I felt as if I was being watched. STOP IT!!!! I screamed in my head. "We are live," Jules announced. Everyone stood still and quiet, for what seemed like an eternity. Waiting. Waiting. Finally, our first set of west coast servers came online and with it over one thousand hospitals. Next, the mid-west hospitals came online, another fifteen hundred. The national map continued to light up as each section came online, and with it, data poured in. Finally, the last state lit up and sighs of relief swept across the room and everyone started cheering. The magnitude of what just occurred was sinking in. After months of hard work and planning, we are finally done with this portion of the project. I know there will be bugs or kinks, whatever, to be worked out. That however is the easy part compared to what we have accomplished over the last few months.

For the first time in weeks, I felt true happiness again. This was my baby as much as it was anyone else's, I was immensely proud to have been a part of it. Also, for the first time in weeks, the misery of another failed relationship was nowhere in sight. My head was swimming and I felt a little off-balance. All I could think of was all the hours of work we had put into making this happen. I am so proud of these people and myself. I have worked with many types of people over the years, but none as committed as we have been. How many people would go a whole month without pay to make sure we stayed on a budget? How many people would have continued to work 40 – 60 + hours a week? These people are my second family, all of which I love and respect. Cannot stand spending too much time with any of them, but like I said, my second family.

All at once, I felt arms around me, Mani was congratulating me and I her on a job well done. "I told you there was nothing to worry about. Now, let us get the interviews over with so we can all celebrate." Mani was all smiles; one smile from Mani could bring any man to his knees. That reporter is in big trouble, and we both knew it.

My portion of the job being done, I was free to return to my solitude. I was not much of one for celebrating these days, besides if I did not hurry and escape it would be too late. I grabbed my things off the desk and headed for the nearest exit. I could hear someone calling my name in the background; I dare not stop, as I was only just a few more feet from freedom. Pushing open the exit door, the sun blared through and I rushed out the door. "Yes!" I practically screamed it. I made it without being stopped. Rushing to my car I shoved all my stuff in through the driver's side door as I climbed in, pulling the car door shut behind me. Slowly and methodically pulling out of my parking space, I continued to forge my way to freedom.

It really was a beautiful day. The sun was shining but the temperature was cool with a slight breeze blowing. My cell started ringing almost immediately; I did not answer it though. Mani would be so pissed that I did not stay for the celebration, but she would understand. I could not be around all those people. I have tried meditation and medication; nothing seemed to help these days. I just want to be left alone. Alone, did I actually think that? Well, you really cannot get more alone than I am, alone in my own head. Now that is a scary thought.

Almost home, one last store before I get there, anything I need? No. I hate going grocery shopping more than anything else. I am so fortunate that they have delivery services now that can deliver whatever you want; groceries, alcohol, anything really. I am in heaven, I thought smiling to myself. I never have to leave home again. I am sure my therapist would find something wrong with that. Kathy is always telling me to put myself out there, get back on the horse. She is all about old clichés. Hell, I have not even ridden a horse in years. I do not care what they say, just because you fall off does not mean you should get back on. Sometimes maybe it is a sign that maybe you should stay off. Guess that is why I fired her and have not bothered to find another to replace her, the therapist, or the ex-girlfriend.

Finally, home. The phone is ringing off the hook, of course. I have no plans to answer that one either. I know it is Mani. I am once more safe from the insanity and confusion that lurks around every corner of the openness outside my home. Sometimes I ask myself, "how did I get here?" "What brought me to this moment in time, where I would rather be alone than to share time with people?" I am not sure how to answer that. I have never really been a very social person. I have always had difficulty fitting in; I did at least try to fit in when I was with someone. Maybe it was my youth when I last felt that I belonged. When I still had Cassie.

Whomever I was with, their friends became my friends, at least for the short time we were together. Oh, sure occasionally one of those friends would continue with me on my journey, but mostly they shifted back to the ex. I had a stronger friendship base in the past. Past is the keyword, smiling as I listen to myself. Indeed, what would my ex-therapist say about all this conversation in my head?

Enough! That is enough. It's time to move onto the next challenge and get my things ready for the trip back home. I do not know why I obsess over the past so much. I know that if we do not reflect on what was wrong, we are doomed to repeat it. How does that work if the things that go wrong are never the same? Everyone has different issues; not all baggage is the same. Baggage, that is what our issues are called nowadays, use to be problems, then issues and now it is baggage. I am tired of dealing with every-one else's baggage. When can you finally let go and just be? What is it that makes life so hard that even loving someone is a chore? Here I go again; it is like a bad rerun that I am destined to play out....

No, truly I am not playing the same rerun repeatedly. I am however replaying my role in what went wrong. I play it through my mind to try to figure out where I went wrong, but it would seem, that my error is the type of person I choose to become involved with. Over-bearing, under-achiever, and over-compensator you name it. Is it fear or shame? What is the real reason for the choices of partners I make? The one thing I do know is I am too tired to keep trying. I guess that is part of the reason why I have become a shut-in, and I really do not like people all that much. Too much fakeness, too much keeping up with the Jones (whoever the hell they are). Just too damn much. I have never understood why people cannot just be themselves. Do people hate themselves so much, or think so little of themselves that they must constantly play the role of someone else, anyone else? Then there is the other. No, I do not want to go there, it will just give me the creeps again. Oh hell, too late.

I must be losing my mind, I feel as though at times someone is watching me, following me, and even when I am alone in my home sleeping, I can feel a presence. I suppose that is the real reason that I hide from the world. I have become scared of my own shadow ever since the assault. My common sense tells me that not everything is what it appears to be. I try to always be rational, keep in mind that I do live in reality most of the time. I laugh to myself, a nervous kind of laughter that sounds unreal to me. If my ex-therapist heard me talk like that, she would have had me committed. Sometimes I would swear that I have seen someone watching me. Out of the corner of my eye I catch a glimpse of a woman, but only for a second. She is always in the shadows, dark and never speaking. I have tried to get her to speak to me. Is she a ghost maybe? Can ghosts talk? I do not know if ghosts talk, but this one does not. She stays in the shadows, just far enough away that I cannot make out any of her features. I do not feel as though she is a threatening spirit. Most of the time, I feel as though she is watching over me, and protecting me. Damn good thing my ex-therapist is not around. Ok, now I am freaking myself out. My breathing and pulse have increased, my eyes dart from one end of the room to the other. My anxiety is increasing, calm down, I tell myself. As I continue to scan the room, I can clearly see that there is nothing or no one there. My breathing slowing first, then my heart rate slowing. This was my life now, moments of panic for no apparent reason. Why? I was not sure, but I refuse to let it rule me forever.

Time to stop this craziness and get packed for my trip back home. What to pack? It may be cool at times, especially when I trek into the mountains. Then the trip to the reservation promises to be a cool day, going even further into the mountains, the higher elevations. Comfortable walking shoes are a must. I do not want to take too much, but then again, I do not want to have to buy anything while I am there. A couple of week's worth of clothes should be enough. I am sure if I wanted to stay longer, my boss would not object. That is not going to happen though. I cannot imagine anything that would cause me to stay away from home longer. Panic is starting to well up in my throat. I can feel the hairs on my neck starting to stand up. Is someone there? I slowly looked around the room holding in my last breath without realizing it. Now slowly letting that breathe out as I see that I am still alone. I continued with packing and thinking of my trip which causes my breathing and pulse to increase again. The thought of having to travel and be around strangers makes me hyperventilate. Slow down, breathe in nice, and slow in through my nose, and out through my mouth. I must find a way to control these episodes. I never used to behave this way. I was once a normal person. If you had told me a few years ago that this is how my life was going to be, I would have told you, you were full of shit. How can so much change in such a short time?

I used to go out with friends, hang out at the beach, and do things in public. Now the thought of being around strangers scares the hell out of me. Strangers scare me a lot more than the thought of a ghost does. I think I would rather be stalked by a ghost in private than be out around people who could touch me either by accident or on purpose. It is not that I have a problem with people as individuals; I have a problem with people in masses. People become unpredictable and act out when they get in groups, add alcohol or drugs and you have a potentially lethal situation. Take people in mob situations, they do things they would normally never think or dream of, destroying property, stealing, or beating someone. There is no way to predict when you will walk into a dire situation, so it is better to stay at home. I know I must sound crazy. How can anyone be so scared of everything all the time? I have to have a pill to wake up in the morning and pill to put me to sleep at night. If I could tolerate the horrible taste of alcohol, I would probably be a drunk.

Well, probably not, as I cannot stand the thought of creating ever bigger issues to deal with than the ones I already have. I don't understand how people become drunks or drug addicts. How can those things possibly make your already stressed-out situation any better? Why waste money on drugs and alcohol when you are already stressing out over lack of money? See the point, it's not a commonsense kind of moment for those people, but what can you do? Good thing I do not have any animals, or I would have to board them, or heaven forbid have someone stay at my house. I cannot stand the thought of someone touching the few things that I have.

Ok, time to get the house in order; all the house plants go onto the porch, make a note to have the mail held for three weeks starting tomorrow (no sense in dealing with junk mail when I first get back), confirm with Corrine that she will stop by every other day while I am away to make sure the house is still standing. I guess that about covers everything...

Chapter Two

Ghost in the shadows

She is so beautiful when she is sleeping. How I long to hold her in my arms and save her from the nightmares. She looks so peaceful when she first falls asleep, then she starts tossing and turning. It is not long before she wakes herself with screaming. I am surprised the neighbors do not call the police when she screams. It sounds as though someone is trying to kill her. What gives her such nightmares? I know nothing of dreams anymore; it has been decades since I have dreamt. No fields of wildflowers or monsters to scare me. How can a monster scare me when I am a monster? Decades have passed since I have known happiness. I have waited patiently for my love to show herself to me. Oh, I have had my simple pleasures. Lusted after others, but none have consumed me the way she does.

When I was young and mortal, I was confident and even a little arrogant. I never allowed anything to stand in the way of what I wanted. I am fortunate that I have had so many years to grow and mellow. Years of having reflected on the mortality of the human spirit, how fragile they are, and how short their lives really are. Nothing lasts forever, even those of us who have the false bravado of being immortal. Even we can be killed, just not like in those crazy fiction movies.

Being here with her like this, I find myself looking

back on the past and seeing the things that I could have done differently. Things that would have improved the lives of others, had I not been so selfish and self-absorbed. She is the first thing I feel I have gotten right in a long time. Saving her, saved me and now I am her protector for the rest of her life. Whether she will choose to love me or scorn my love for her, I will protect her with my life. Someone such as her should be out living life and seeing the world. I want to do that for her. I want to share a world with her free of fear and full of life.

How could I possibly come into her life right now, so many things uncertain? My world is about to burst at the seams, and I dare not open her up to that. No, this has to be enough. The moments that I watch over her, for now, this will have to be enough.

What is she doing? Why does she keep herself locked away so much? I never have difficulty finding her as she is usually at home. I should have killed that man, who assaulted her and torn him to shreds. She is so beautiful and was so full of life. I stay in the background, her protector. She thinks I am a ghost and that is all we can have for now. I can feel something big coming, something that will change our lives forever. My world is not safe for her, nor is her own world. But I will protect her from both for as long as I can. Where is she going in such a hurry? I can feel her anxiety welling up, as her breathing quickens. I feel as though I should introduce myself to her, but how? "Hi, I am the crazed woman who nearly killed the man who attacked you in the parking lot that day." "No, I wasn't scared. You see I am a vampire." Oh, yeah, I can see where that would go over really well. NOT! She would probably run screaming into the night and get hit by a car or something. No, it is better that I stay behind the scenes for now. We will have our moment; of that I am sure. I have not lived over 300 hundred years for nothing. Her car has stopped. So, I pull over, making sure that I am out of her sight. Looking around I can see that she has just gone into her workplace. She rarely shows up here so this must be a special day. There are definitely a lot of cars in the parking lot. She should be fine here for now. Besides, I know where I can easily find her later. She will be at home. Now, it is time for me to return home, at least for a couple of days.

Chapter Three

Issues of the Old Ones

"No, I refuse to leave it alone. We have been down this road before. Everyone knows that we do not make obvious kills. Hell, we don't even have to kill at all anymore." Shantini was screaming at the counsel. "Someone needs to get these newbies under control. How dare they put the rest of us in jeopardy?" Shantini continued to rant. "I agree, who is the creator of these restless and ignorant children?" Deshale's voice echoed through the chamber, dark and sinister. There was no mistaking who was speaking, and the crowd became silent. Deshali is the oldest recognized Vampire of our day. He is over a thousand years old and has been through wars; both vampire and human. He is the strongest, most agile, and most cunning of all the vampires. "I do not believe that anyone has spoken up to claim them as of yet," Katherine stated. "However, the fact remains that they must be dealt with. Humans do not want to acknowledge what goes bump in the night. It is too frightening for them. I do not wish to become hunted out of fear and stupidity." The room murmured with consensus, "indeed, why should the rest of us have to suffer due to others' transgressions?" Emilia's voice, light and beautiful floated across the room. "It would seem appropriate that they are hunted down and extinguished. I will volunteer to become one of the groups that put the rabid mongrels out of our misery."

Once again, the room fell silent; no one wanted to be on either end of the hunt. Killing another Vampire was sacrilegious to us. We know how to get rid of our own, but for humans, the skill, speed and strength are too much. Eventually, they would hunt them down, but not without losing many people and exposing us in the process.

Deshali stayed silent observing the varied responses around the room. He was not one to make snap judgments or escalate a situation without first knowing what the probable outcome would be. He also did not want the same hunters forming groups and alliances that could become dangerous in the future. The quicker the problem was handled the better. There was only one that he knew without a doubt could be trusted to do the job and not turn on their own later, Katherine. She was an extremely complicated woman, who by her build and demeanor that was a sight for anyone to behold. She had fought her way through many battles to become the woman she is today.

Katherine is an immensely powerful and skillful hunter. Once she has decided on her prey, they had no chance of escaping. Deshali had seen her hunt and kill. She had a skill that even Deshali did not possess, nor would Deshali want to be on the receiving end of. She was a rarity; a human that had been turned that possessed all the talents of those before her and all the brutality. She had fought with her demons and won. She now had total control over the elements and herself. Deshali never imagined when he turned her that she would turn out to be all that she has become, Deshali smiled to himself.

"I agree, now is the time to deal with this situation before it spirals out of control." Deshali stated with such conviction that no one could mistake his meaning. "Katherine will be the lead. Everyone involved will take their orders directly from her and no one else. If you cannot follow her, then do not volunteer." Everyone knew Deshali's word as law; he was with the revolution that took the vampires out of the darkness and into the light. No one wanted to go back to that, at least no one here. The laws were basic:

1. Do not kill without provocation, or for sport.

2. Do not allow our secrets to be known to those that are not like us or to those that are not with us.

3. Breaking the law is death.

The days of being hunted down as animals had ended; however, a threat to return to the old ways always lingers in the subconscious, at least for those that lived through it. Back in the days when Katherine was a fresh vampire, she remembered the hunger and the blood lust. If it were not for Deshali she would never have made it through, at least that is what she believes. Deshali was the most sensitive and compassionate during Katherine's changing. Do not get it wrong; Deshali was also the most demanding and the most overbearing; however, Deshali did know it was for Katherine's benefit. When Deshali talks everyone listens, he has the wisdom of centuries behind him as well as the knowledge from formal and informal education. Katherine remembered as a child, wishing that she could have been like her Uncle Deshali.

"Now who will volunteer? Do not take this job lightly, the newbies may not have the skill that many of you possess, but they make up for it in their brutality and speed. Besides, their minds are linked, so be careful about raiding their nests. They are like a fine-tuned machine when it comes to working as one." Katherine continued to inform those that volunteered. By the end of the night, there were two groups of ten. Katherine starts to strategize. "In the event that we are not able to get them all and if they scatter, it is imperative that you use this." Katherine pulled out a small dart-like object. "This is a tracker; it will track around the world if necessary. It bounces off the satellites. If you cannot kill them, tag them so we can finish the job later. They will never know they have been tagged it burrows under their skin. If you even think, one may get away, tag 'em. Once you encounter one, do not underestimate him or her. Innocence is one of the ways the newbies get what they need. Remember when you were first turned, it was like a drug, one that you want to keep taking. Worse than any synthetic drug made, they will fight to the end to live. Make no mistake, vampire or human, death is the only thing they believe in. Go for the heart and then for decapitation, once you have done both then you can slow down. Appropriately discard of the body and head by setting it on fire. Always stay in pairs, one discarding the body, and the other watching for more vampires. Once you have finished with the discarding of the body, check-in and get your next assignment. Under no circumstances do you leave the body without discarding of it properly. Any questions? NO? Good." "One last thing, failure is not an option." Katherine finished.

There was no noise; you could have heard a pin drop as Katherine started handing out the information packets. Everyone was focused. Everyone knew what was at stake here, their whole way of life. If the masses of humans ever found out that they existed, it would be genocide all over again. People, who fear, try to exterminate what they fear the most, THEM. Those among them who have centuries behind them knew what the witch hunts were like. Those of them who have lived long enough know what it is like to be tracked down and exterminated. The only way they survived was in letting them think they had ridden the world of them, many of them were gone. No, failure was not an option; Katherine was playing through the past in her mind, and memories she would have just as soon forgotten. Once this is over, we can go back to our lives, I can go back to her... Katherine rarely allowed herself to become distracted, but the thought of her definitely had that effect on her. Her mind had been wondering way too much these days, she was glad she will be able to see her soon... But for now, she needed to focus.

The latest intel Katherine had was that one set of Newbies was in the Smokey Mountains in Tennessee; the others were in Cherokee, North Carolina. She had no idea why these two places were chosen, but that is where they were going. It was way to close to close to home for Katherine. Shantini will take her group to North Carolina. Obviously, her group will be in Tennessee. Once the job is done, everyone will meet at Katherine's house in Pigeon Forge, for a debriefing. By then, Katherine should have more information as to whether there are other nests, which would require their attention. Deshalei would be checking into what has already leaked and find a way to "fix it". Once he had a clearer picture, we would know what is left to be taken care of. Deshali, Shantini and Katherine looked at each knowing what was meant by "left to be taken care of". Katherine thought to herself the one who started this whole mess.

Chapter Four

Long trip

Wow, it is time to head out. List in hand; making sure that I have taken care of everything before I get on the road. Oh, damn almost forgot to call Corrine. Damn it, I hate voice mail especially when people have long recordings or those crazy joke recordings. "Corrine its Ash. I am getting ready to leave. I put the plants on the front porch. The alarm is set, and the back gate is locked. Hope you remember the code to turn off the alarm and don't forget where I hid the spare key. See everyone in a couple of weeks." Guess that covered everything. Ok, ready to hit the interstate. Guess I will fill up down the road, hopefully, gas will be cheaper. Shit! dropped my phone between the seats. Of course, it would start ringing. I will just have to call them back when I stop for gas. Eight hours to go, ugh…. Eight hours to sit and mull over the events of the years gone by, to trudge up old memories. To analyze, scrutinize, and criticize old decisions, oh what a joy. However, my mind was not letting me open that vault, the one with all the failed relationships and dreadful choices I had made in the past. Something else was in the way, something was holding that vault closed so tightly today, even dynamite could not have opened it. What is going on inside my head? I had no idea; except I had a feeling that bad things were coming, and I should be very scared. I spent a lot of my time being scared these days, scared of my own shadow as it were. Today is not one of those days. Something had taken hold of me and refused to allow the old anxiety to creep in, to take hold and cripple me. At least for now, I was at peace. I turned on the radio and listened to the oldies channel for as long as I could make out the words. Then I would scan through the channels for more oldies stations. I continued this way for the duration of the trip not really thinking or even feeling anything. I was relieved. Looking down at the gas hand, I realized I needed to make another stop, and surprising this did not fill me with dread. What was happening? It was like I was going home. I was going home, but that was not the home I meant. It was like I was going to the home that fills you with calm, love and a sense of completeness. I had not ever felt this feeling and yet here it was. Something big was coming and I knew it deep in the back of my mind, but nothing registered right away for this feeling of euphoria had entered the picture that refused to allow any bad thoughts past. It was as though someone else had taken up space in my brain and insisted that it be a happy place. For once my mind was calm.

Guess I am destined to overthink everything, but for now, I needed gas, or I would be walking. Great gas for 2.50 a gallon, woohoo. Now, where is that damn phone? Ok, who called? My brother, he probably wants to know if I left yet. "Hey brother, what's up?" "Just calling to make sure you are still coming up" he sounded tired. "Yes, I am filling up my tank now. I am going to the cabin first to rest, and then I will see you tomorrow or the next day." I stated. "Ok, I was hoping you had changed your mind about the cabin and was gonna stay at my house. Oh, well as long as you are coming." He sounded disappointed. "Yeah, well you have a house full already and I need some down-time. Besides, I haven't been to the mountains in ages." My brother was always good at guilt trips, but this time it was not going to work. A few more minutes of chit chat, and I decided it was time to get going. Just a couple more hours then finally, at the cabin. It is a gorgeous place. I have always loved it in the mountains. The air is so fresh and clean.

I remember as a child looking forward to spring break because that meant we would be going camping in the mountains. The last year we camped as a family: my mom, dad, sister and brother; it was unusually cold, and we took extra blankets to keep warm. The morning after we set up camp was a little foggy, but there was no mistaking the commotion taking place a few campsites away. People were laughing and talking loudly, my dad warned us to stay away from the noise if we did not want to be tossed out by the ranger, so we started towards the mountain stream until we heard a loud growl and the sound of thunder. A huge brown bear was barreling its way down the side of the mountain. At first, it looked as though it were charging someone. However, once all the people were out of the way it was easy to see two cubs trying to get into the trashcans. The big bear slowed down once everyone had moved further away from the cubs. We were a good distance away, but mom hurried us into the bathroom. The park ranger making his rounds, showed up as the bears were heading up the opposite side of the park. My dad was so mad, "stupid tourist gonna get the rest of us killed just so they can see bear cubs. Damn it, can't they just go to the zoo." We burst out laughing. Finally, mom allowed us to leave the bathroom, thank goodness because my brother let out the smelliest fart. My sister and I ran screaming and laughing, with him chasing after us. The things you remember, I had not thought about that day in ages, the last time we were ever a real family. We did not have much in those days, but we had each other.

Why didn't I take a plane? Oh yea, I would have been at the mercy of my family. No alone time. Oh hell to the no on that one. I am so ready for the solitude of nature. I am glad I had the caretaker to turn on the lights and heat for me, it was getting quite chilly. I am so exhausted; cannot imagine I will have much trouble falling asleep tonight.

The cabin is a beautiful 2-story log cabin, with a fully enclosed wraparound porch, which is located on the side of a mountain, so when you step onto the back porch, you get a majestic view down the mountainside. If you are fond of heights, the balcony on the second floor can give you more of a view. There is a hot tub on the back porch, I make sure to turn it on before unpacking. I want the water to be nice and hot while I am unloading the car. After 8 hours of driving, I can use the time in a hot tub. These portable hot tubs are nice; this one is big enough for four people. My muscles are starting to ache all over, so I am ready for some downtime. The temperature must have dropped 20 degrees in the last 10 minutes; I have put my coat on. I love it up here. Thank goodness for the care-taker, the cabin is nice and toasty. Three pieces of luggage, One computer and a bag of snacks. I am done unpacking and ready to climb into the hot tub. Strange for the last couple of days I have not felt like I was being watched, it is a strange sensation to feel as though you have lost your guardian angel. I am not sure how I feel about that.

The next day, I decided to take a hike in the mountains to clear my head, I needed some time and some space to myself. I have always loved this time of the year, the leaves had long since changed color, browns and tans, even some reds. The air was crisp and refreshing, I found myself stopping frequently just to inhale my surroundings. The sound of the spring water traveling down the river was very soothing. The birds seemed to have their own language as I heard them often chattering above me. My mind kept creeping back to this last catastrophe of a relationship, we should have stayed friends. My mind kept working over the relationship, what happened? Nothing that was the problem. It never progressed into more than friends with benefits at least for her, but it did end badly. She was young and selfish. I always felt as though I was not a priority for her, and that is true because I was not. We went from talking constantly, in person or on the phone (for months), to barely seeing each other. This type of behavior would eventually cause one of us to say to hell with it and end it. Months would go by and we would not see or hear from each other. Then one weak moment, either hers or mine and before you know it there, we were again, usually ending in the bedroom with some mind-blowing sex. Do you know the definition of crazy? Well, I believe it should be repeating the same behaviors, and expecting a different outcome. She was like a drug to me, I hated that I wanted her. I hated that I needed her but could not stop myself. Damn, I needed an intervention. It would not have mattered, my sister tried time and time again to make me see the insanity. Of course, I saw the insanity; went to sleep with it and woke up with it. It did not help though. I am not sure what she got out of it, was I just someone to fill the loneliness until she met the one, she really wanted to be with? Did she ever really care, or was love just her way of saying hello and goodbye? It still stings, just as much as it did the last time I laid eyes on her. I can feel the tears welling up in my eyes, that burn you feel just before the first tear falls and a flood of emotion takes over, and the tears are falling like rain. I want to run or scream anything to make the pain stop, but it never does. Every day the pain is a reminder of the poor choices I have made in trying to find **THE ONE**. The one that makes your heart skip a beat when she walks into the room or the sound of her voice fills you with joy. For a solitary moment in time, I have been fortunate enough to steal a glimpse at what that feels like. Sometimes I think that is what saddens me the most, that I will never find the one who sees in me what I see in her.... I hate it when my thoughts get away from me, especially when I am walking in an unfamiliar area.

Thank goodness for the asphalt trail, only when I was younger did I enjoy trekking across the bare country. Those days had long since come and gone especially since, I really was not paying much attention to where I was going other than following the premade trail. The thought of breaking a bone or twisting my ankle did not appeal to me. Nowadays, I enjoyed long walks on the beach back home. Florida was still warm and walking on the southernmost beaches was still possible. The weather was so freakish that it never felt like the holidays. Snow during the winter; not likely.

Chapter Five

The Moment

The beginning, the moment true insanity took over. When she stole my heart away. The most beautiful woman I have ever seen or thought I saw? At times, I am not sure that the events as I am going to describe even happened. It was at times like a never-ending nightmare. Her hair was black as the darkest of nights. Her eyes were as green as emeralds. I remember thinking, "I could drown in those eyes," laughing to myself. Her skin was the color of ivory. She had the whitest teeth I have ever seen and a little menacing. She took my breath away, just the mere sight of her. The first time we met it was in the fall I had gone back home for a visit.

As I was walking up the trail, lost in my thoughts, I practically ran into her. "You might want to pay closer attention to where you're going. It can be quite dangerous up here, if you don't" she stated, her voice was as smooth as silk and I felt my skin tingle as though she had just caressed my cheek with her hand. She was wearing a tan polo shirt and a pair of jeans with hiking shoes (that looked quite expensive). The shirt was form-fitting so you could see a luscious set of breasts and well-formed biceps underneath. I felt such a strange sensation in the pit of my stomach. I realized now that was the moment, I fell in love with her. "Oh, I'm sorry. I guess I was a little preoccupied." I said almost in a stutter. She just smiled and continued on her way, I watched after her until she was out of sight. When I could no longer see her, I felt lost and had the overwhelming urge to follow her. At first, I was walking slowly, not even realizing that I was picking up speed on the way down. Before I knew it, I was at an all outrun. Surely, I did not pass her, I would have seen her, right? I stopped suddenly, "what was that noise? Did someone scream? Ok, stop it I am just scaring myself now". I started walking again and decided I needed to get out of there. I cannot believe I decided to take a hike this late. The sun had all but set. There was barely enough light to see the trail. Damn, I hate driving in the dark, trying to keep my mind off the fact that I was alone out here in the middle of nowhere. Now I know that was a scream! I felt like I should run away, but I found myself heading towards the screaming.

Not knowing what direction the sound was coming from, I allowed my instinct to take over and lead me, right into her. "We need to stop meeting like this before people start to talk," she stated sarcastically as she grabbed me to keep us both from falling over. Her hands were so warm and inviting. I found myself wanting her. "Oh, I'm sorry. I thought I heard someone screaming and thought I could possibly help."

Her skin smells so good like freshly made cotton candy. I could feel the warmth of her arms surrounding me. She had not released me. I raised my eyes to meet hers. My head began to swim, and I felt a little faint. She must have realized that for her grip on me tightened. I should have been afraid, but I was not. She was like a Greek Goddess....

"I heard the scream, too. It was just some kids acting foolish over there trying to scare the shit out of each other", she stated, smiling, but it never reached her eyes. There was coldness in them that gave me a chill. I could not keep myself from staring at her; I was drawn to her like bees to honey. She was so perfect: her breasts, her legs, every single inch of her was perfect. "You plan on standing here all night?" she seemed to be getting agitated, "No, it's definitely time to get out of here, this place gives me the creeps at night." I was sure my voice was trembling. "In that case, I will walk you to your car. My friends should be down the trail shortly," she stated quite unpleasantly. Her change in attitude was starting to annoy me. "That would be nice, but I don't want to take you away from your group. Thank you for the offer though." Even if she wanted to be rude, I would not allow myself to be. I turned and walked away making every effort not to turn around and glare at her. I was getting more annoyed by the minute. My last girlfriend was like that, she would get pissy about everything she felt she had to do, meaning things she would volunteer for, but really did not want to do. How dare she? Who was to say she wasn't running into me? That's what happens when you step out from nowhere. It was getting dark and difficult to see. I was fuming when I felt a tug at my elbow. "I said I would walk you down", her grip tightening on my elbow. I was so surprised by her strength that I found myself obeying her. "I am quite capable of walking without your assistance" I tossed at her. "Well, I am not so sure about that" she said. I felt my temper getting the best of me. "I don't care how strong you are; you can let me go, NOW!" I demanded stopping so abruptly, I thought she would pull my arm out of its socket. "You didn't really think you could escape my grip, now did you?" my anger flaring again with the obvious laughter in her voice. "I told you to let me go; besides there is my car. So technically, you did your part. So, fucking let go of my arm," my anger getting the better of me. I attempted to yank my arm away from her. She just laughed, as she loosened her grip on my arm but did not let go completely. "Looks like you have some anger issues. Which is very rude considering I volunteered to walk you to your car"? That was it, "who the hell do you think you are. You offered, but I never accepted. Next thing I know I am being "man-handled" and practically dragged to my car", I felt the grip on my arm begin to tighten, but I didn't care, no one was going to talk to me like that especially when she was the one being rude.... I have had enough of people treating me any way they want. Before I could say another word her arms were around me pulling me close to her. I felt the heat of her chest against mine as my I sucked in the air my breasts pushed against her; her lips came down on mine with such force as to part mine. I felt her wet tongue find its way into my mouth demanding attention. Her lips softened on mine and the kiss became more sensual and gentler as her tongue explored my mouth. Her arms engulfed me, like a protective blanket surrounding me; I felt so safe and wanted. I pressed closer, wanting more. The heat of our bodies seems to elevate higher and I could feel the dampness forming between us, the sweat soaking our clothes. My body was begging for more when it had finished as quickly as it began. "I would suggest that you relieve some of that tension next time before trying to pick a fight with a total stranger. I could have taken you right here and you would have let me." She said with a huge smile on her face, she was so full of herself, but I could not deny the reaction my body had to her touch. There was nothing I could say, except "Whatever," with as much venom as I could muster. Before she could say another word, I was in my car, and slamming the door (something told me however that if she had wanted me to stay, I would have been helpless to leave). I looked in my rearview mirror to find her laughing. Laughing, how dare her. I am practically assaulted, and she finds it funny. I was way too familiar with people like her, taking their liberties at someone else's expense. My anger made for a short drive back. By the time, I had over analyzed this encounter and scrutinized every "worthless relationship" I had over the last ten years I was fuming. I am generally "the glass is half full" kind of girl, but after this last relationship and the past few years, I guess it has left me kind of jaded. What the fuck? I must be from another planet because I definitely do not get people. Say what you mean, mean what you say. How fucking hard is that? That is all I want to know. How fucking hard is that? I love you today, but to hell with you tomorrow if I see someone who interests me more. What is this? A fucking bargain basement sale, if I do not like the fit let us just throw it out and try on another? Whom the fuck made that kind of thing okay? I am a person, with real feelings that can be hurt. I cannot remember who said the expression, but it so applies "if you cut me, do I not bleed?" "Yeah, I bleed motherfucker; now leave me the hell alone!" Why did every encounter have to end with me feeling like this?

Over halfway down I started getting carsick and had to stop on the side of the road. I did not dare get out of the car; I just knew that crazed woman was waiting to pounce to prove that she was in control. I sat still more out of anger than anything else, even fear. My body had responded to her like to no one ever before. I had no control of myself, and she was right she could have done anything she wanted to me and I would have been helpless to stop her. It was as if I had no mind in this body which is the way most of my relationships got started. My brain apparently went on vacation and forgot to leave a memo. Finally, the nausea slowly subsided, so I continued down the mountain.

When I reached the town, I remembered that I did not have any real food at the cottage, only snacks. I decided to stop at the store on the way home. I hate grocery stores more than I hate assholes that think they are all that I laughed to myself. She definitely was one "hot" woman though.

Damn, even at this time of night, the grocery store is packed. I am really a recluse. I always say, "I am not racist, I am an equal opportunity hater, and I hate everyone equally" Well not really but when I am pissed off it sounds good. Ok, in and out, I will run in, get what I need and get out. Just that simple: milk, eggs, cereal, bread and lunch-meat, that is it. It is amazing what you can live on when you are alone. Sometimes I hate the thought of having to eat at all. UGH... Too many people and, too much noise make for a very grumpy woman. My head was starting to pound. Come on, how long does it take to get a price check? I hate having to stand in line, to feel like cattle moving to be slaughtered.... All the strange people come out at night. Hell, look at me. The man behind me smelled like moth-balls, that musty odor that gets in your nose and makes you want to rip your head off. The large woman that was in front of me smells sweaty and almost moldy. Ok, Lord help me get out of here. Finally, the line is moving. I acknowledge the need for people who do this type of job; however, there should be an age limit. I am of the thought that you are either too old or too young to be working at a supermarket. That is just my opinion. At 80 years old, which is what that woman looked like is definitely too old to be a cashier. Oh, MY GOD! I thought I would never escape. Crawling in bed at midnight is not my ideal situation but going to the store first thing in the morning would be a "going postal" moment for me.

What an evening it turned out to be, meeting a gorgeous woman (who pissed me off) who if not for the attitude would have been the woman of my dreams. Time to get ready for some sleep. Turned on the TV for background noise; I get so nervous when it is too quiet. I cannot take it too quiet or too noisy for that matter. My mind will start to wonder, and I could swear I heard something in the quiet, something menacing.

It is so dark and cold here, where am I, how did I get here? I am so cold, so very cold.... A foreboding comes over me and I froze with fear. I cannot move. "Help!" I screamed at the top of my lungs. "Someone please help me!" I continued to yell despite knowing that no one was going to answer. There was only silence and darkness. I yelled and screamed until I no longer could. What was going to happen to me? This was scaring the hell out of me. No sounds. No wind blowing. No traffic noises. Nothing else: but silence and the musky smell of damp earth. It was so dark. Running my hand along the wall, I felt a sticky wetness beneath my fingertips. My feet were soaked. Was the ground wet as well, was I standing in water?

Oh, my goodness, did I hear that right, I reached over half asleep and turned the TV up:

"A young woman found dead at the base of the waterfalls, no ID yet, and the police are not saying much. Some are speculating that she was around 25-30 years old. A tourist most likely, best estimation put her time of death around dusk or shortly thereafter." The newscaster had said in a very sorrowful voice.

At the waterfall, which waterfall? No, it could not have been the waterfall I had left earlier. There was no one else around, I surely would have noticed. Except for that annoying woman. My thoughts drifted to her sensual lips and the taste of her mouth. Her scent was intoxicating; I remember feeling breathless while I was with her. Ok, snap out of it, I demanded to myself. There are several water-falls up there and some are extremely dangerous. I barely had time to turn the TV down before sleep took over again, please do not let me dream.

.... It is so very cold here, I remembered thinking to myself. What is that smell? Like death? My heart skipped a beat, fear started to rise from the pit of my stomach. Oh, MY GOD! What was that...? There was only silence and darkness. I yelled and screamed until I no longer could. What was going to happen to me? This was scaring the hell out of me. No sounds. No wind blowing. No traffic noises. Nothing else: but silence and the musky smell of damp earth. It was so dark...

The same dream that had haunted me for months. I would not have been so bothered by it, except for the fact that my dreams have a way of coming true, at least the bad ones. Like the one about Cassie, my sweet Cassie...

So why am I like this? Staying away from people and places. As best I can recall it started one evening on my way home. I stopped off at Super Wal-Mart (which was my fa-vorite store) to pick up a few things. On the way out to my car, I was attacked, if that's what you would call it. I had a strange feeling for a while of being watched, probably had nothing to do with this incident. I was walking out to my car and someone tried to grab my purse punching me at the same time. I am not very sure about everything that happened after that but I have been having issues ever since. I was told that a dark-haired stranger took the assailant down and practically killed him in the process. I have no memory of the event just a sense of fear and dread; obviously, a feeling that took up residence and decided never to leave.

If it were not for this forced vacation, I would still have been at home. I had not seen my family and friends up here in such a long time. My boss was determined that I was working too much, what does a boss care if you are working too much. Well, this one happens to be my good friend, so there you go. I had not been on a real vacation in a couple of years now. The most recent cancellations were due to always managing to find some reason not to go. My cat needs surgery and I can't afford to board her (of course I did not have a cat and still don't), or I went out hiking and twisted my ankle (thus not hiking on rough terrain anymore). Anything and everything was becoming an excuse for me not to leave my home, I barely managed to make it to the grocery store these days, thank God for delivery.

I just do not understand what the big deal is, everything I need I can get delivered or do without. Working from home is so much more convenient. It had been a while since I worked from anywhere else other than home. I could even get all my continuing education credits online, as well as having someone come into my home for clinical and practical application of whatever I was learning in school these days. I am amazed that anyone ever leaves home.

Sometimes I get restless, call up a friend or two and go out. It is generally easier to blend in when I am distracted by conversation. Good food and good company have always been something I have cherished, the only times that I can exist outside, in a world that constantly separates us from each other. Separation due to class, education, money, and body size are just the beginnings. Crazy, how your mind works.

What to do today? I was supposed to contact my family as soon as I arrived, but I am not in the mood to be bombarded with questions, just yet. I know they mean well, but there is only so much endless chatter I can take. Ok, the family later, I stated to myself as if trying to keep a promise that I would call them later. So, what now, a shower? That is always a good place to start. I hate waiting for hot water which is the one thing I like about hotels; the water is always instantly hot. Stripping off my clothes I climbed into the shower, I can't get my mind off that young woman dying in the mountains yesterday. Her family must be crazed with grief by now. Fortunately, death is one of those times when people tend to rise above their faults and come together to support those who have lost someone. Well, generally speaking anyway, unless of course, you are one of those Jerry Springer rejects (so far down on the food chain they start to eat each other).

The water is so hot but rejuvenating. Maybe I will go to some of the local shops, there is not anything that I want to buy but it would be nice to look around. I stopped collecting knick-knacks quite a while ago, not good to hold on to too many physical aspects of life as it can be so short-lived. Then I will call my family and some friends to arrange dinner plans. I really must contact everyone; they would be so upset if I came and went without seeing anyone which would really be my preference. Soaked, I climb out of the shower, grabbing one of the towels off the hanger. After drying off, I put on some comfy pants, a tank top, and a pullover sweater with a pair of scandals. Gently pulling my hair back into a ponytail I wrapped a scrunchy around the handful of hair, throw on some eye makeup and I am ready to go. Oh, the air feels so nice, just a little bit of a chill in the air that should go away as the day progresses (I hope).

The traffic is not too bad for this time of the morning, just a few cars. Crossing a four-lane highway for some could be quite traumatic if the traffic were more congested. Shops line both sides of the highway, but the ones that I prefer, of course, would be on the opposite side. The first shop was a glass trinket shop. Little delicate figurines made from blown glass with a mixture of colors tinting them. The woman behind the counter is not that friendly, not like most of the clerks or cashiers in the other shops normally are. She definitely falls into "it's all about me", from her self-absorbed attitude to the way she judges all her customers as they leisurely stroll in. Bleach blonde hair flowing down her back. Her eyes are the strangest color, colored contacts no doubt. She seems like a 30 something, trying to be 20 something. What a shame that she is so self-absorbed, I bet if she smiled her face would crack. Probably not, but one can hope. I have definitely had enough of her negative energy and this shop. Walking out the door, I hear her grunt in disapproval. Whatever, why would I buy anything from her? People are so strange. I have decided to forgo the next couple of shops; I am not really interested in tacky t-shirt shops. Finally, I find the shop I was looking for, an average-sized place with stripes of red and white, reminds me of a candy cane. I love visiting this place, it is a candy factory. The machines are just getting started with the candy maker putting the taffy on the pulling machine. It smells so good in here.

I can remember when I was a child and my mom would bring us here and get each of us one piece of our favorite candy. The smell of this place never changes; standing here, I closed my eyes and remembered happier times. My sister running over to me, saying "I am going to get a nut cluster this time, not the chocolate covered raisins", and then when it is her time to order she of course always gets the chocolate covered raisins. My brother on the other hand, would get wrapped taffy in different flavors so he could get rid of the ones he did not like the flavors of. My favorite is not really candy, but has candy on it, a caramel apple with nuts.

Ok, time to collect a few things and move on. As I arrive at the cashier, a pleasant little twenty-something, natural blonde with the prettiest brown eyes, takes my order and smiles such a beautiful smile; it would easily drop any man to his knees begging for mercy. The woman behind me starts getting agitated, I missed her initial interaction with the other cashier, an older woman with salt and pepper colored hair and very attractive. I can't take my eyes off her lips, so supple and moist. Most people are drawn to beautiful people; I am drawn to beautiful body parts. The rude woman is starting to get irate; I turned to look at her, she venomously yells, "What are you looking at?" I stated, "I am not sure yet, looks like an ass standing by itself." At which point she storms out of the shop. The attractive woman behind the counter mouths the words "thank you"; I responded with; your welcome and completed my order. The young twenty-something has a grin covering her face. What an absolutely beautiful smile.

Enough shopping, I am officially tired of people for now. I think I will go for a hike in the mountains. What are the chances I would run into that woman again. She is probably just a tourist. Ok, enough of that. Damn, time to cross the highway again, this time the traffic has picked up slightly. Crossing at the crosswalk was the only option at this point. Pushing the button at the corner, I decided to try and be patient. Not working too well at this point. As the light changes a black Mercedes with the darkest tinted windows, I have ever seen screeches to a halt missing me by mere inches. I turn toward the vehicle and give my most vicious look at the driver who proceeds to mouth "I am sorry" and threw his hands up in the air. I shook my head and walked away, relieved that I did not wet my pants. I continued crossing the street and heard her yell "I told you, you couldn't be trusted to your own devices", I froze in my tracks. I could not even turn around for fear I would stumble over my own feet. Next thing I know I am being picked up and carried. "Put me down!" I am scream-ing, the people around me laughing and pointing. "Not to worry, she does this all the time," I could hear, laughter in her silky voice. All at once, I am tossed inside the Merce-des, granted the fall was short-lived and relatively pain-less, but the fury that was rising inside me was going to be hell. "What the hell do you think you are doing?" my tone was low but there was no doubt as to my meaning. "I thought I would save the other drivers from running you down," her tone was light and silky. I wanted so much to continue to be angry, but I could feel the heat of anger slip-ping away. "Who are you?" I was truly puzzled at why this woman would make me her personal rescue mission; she did not even know my name. "Ashley, right?" she paused waiting for me to answer. "What? How could you possibly know my name?" I was becoming frightened, the hair on the back of my neck started to stand on end. "Well, considering you tried to run me over yesterday and you had a nameplate on the front of your car. Hello?" sarcasm was dripping from her lips. What beautiful lips she had, so supple and inviting. My mind is beginning to fog. All at once, all I could think of was her: what was her name? What was that beautiful scent emanating from her? Would she kiss me again, and not stop this time? Oh, how I longed for her tongue in my mouth, and her hands caressing my body. What was happening to me? I looked at her for direction, she was smiling, suddenly I was at peace, sinking further into the seat and feeling like I never wanted to leave.

"So now Ashley, you were going to ask me a question?" she paused briefly for an answer. "My name is Katherine" she stated as though I had asked her a question, but I did not. "What? I'm sorry..." my voice trailed off as I pondered this feeling coming over me. What power she had over me. Gazing at her I realized she had a slight smile forming, next thing I know I heard the soft sound of laughter coming from her as her eyes were locked on mine. At the sound of her voice, my mind slowly returned to where I was and what had just transpired, I could say nothing; I had no response, at least for that moment. Once it began to sink in that I was now at her mercy, I became furious. "So now that I am officially your protector, I suppose we should spend some time getting to know one another," she stated as a matter of fact. "Why should we do that?" I questioned; however my curiosity was peaked, and I really did want to know more about her. "Because I said so," she stated, as though her words were law. "Who the fuck do you think you are?" I demanded. "I do not know you, nor do I want to get to know someone as arrogant and full of herself as you are!" I stated as a matter of fact. "How dare you think that you have the right to force yourself upon me or anyone else for that matter!" At this point I was on a role, or so I thought. Then suddenly, she reached over, took my face in her hand, and pulled me to within inches of her face. Her eyes were startling and grew dark, from anger I suppose. "Who are you to judge me? You are just a mere woman who cannot even keep herself safe," she stated, sounding only mildly annoyed. "I am the one you are choosing to intrude upon with your selfish attitude" I flung back with as much disgust as I could manage. I could feel her breath against my face; she held my face captive with her hand. "Why should it matter to you? Why does it bother you so much?" she sounded surprised. "I have been hurt by people that thought that they have a right to treat people any way they feel like, and it didn't seem to matter to them that others suffer because of their selfishness." "Why should others suffer at your whim?" I was thinking of a time when I loved so deeply and was so viscously betrayed. As I stared into her eyes, I felt such sadness, another one of those, it was definitely time to go. "I would appreciate it if you would release my face," I stated without emotion. "Also, pull over here and allow me to leave" I was void of emotion. I could feel myself shutting down. I could no longer tolerate being in the presence of anyone who would show such a complete lack of concern for the feelings of another human being. She reluctantly released my face and motioned for the driver to pull over and stop the car. Her eyes distant, as though she was contemplating what I had just said like it was the first time she had ever heard such a thing. "You are a very strange young woman" she looked genuinely confused. "Strange, how?" My curiosity getting the better of me as I questioned her. "You have taken the pain that someone caused you and externalized it to the whole world. Do you hate everyone, even yourself? I did not see that at first, in the forest, I was confused by your happiness, being that you were alone. I had mistaken you for someone who was waiting for someone. When I walked you to your car and you just left, I was taken aback for a moment. Now, I see that your fear of being hurt again has shut you off from the world. Driver, continue to our destination, our guest will be joining us after all." Her voice sounded different, menacing almost. "I have no intention of going anywhere with you or anyone else for that matter, now stop and let me out", I demanded, starting to feel queasiness in the pit of my stomach. Something was wrong, very wrong. What had just happened? I searched my mind for something to say, "Look my family is waiting for me; I really don't have time for this." I had not had time to call them yet, I hope she didn't realize I was bluffing. "Well, that makes all the difference," she laughed, and the driver gave a weary smile, but the car never slowed down. What was going on? Why would she continue, what did my company mean to her?

"What do you prefer to eat? Meat? Pasta? Any preference?" she asked without really expecting an answer. "What? I want you to pull over and let me out" I stated. "Not an option. I am enjoying your company, such as it is." her lips making a slight grin around the edges as she spoke.

"Are you insane? I mean really, are you insane?" I was very confused. "Why would you want someone's company that doesn't want yours?" I contemplated this question to myself. Hadn't I been guilty of that? Haven't we all been guilty of that at some point in our lives? "Look, I understand if you are having a hard time entertaining yourself but kidnapping someone is not the way to remedy that." I snapped sarcastically, but the car continued. Sitting back in the seat, I noticed just how roomy the vehicle was.

At first, it did not appear roomy, probably since she was practically sitting on top of me. All at once, I thought "ok at the next red light I will just get out" what can she do? Nothing. "I wouldn't advice that" she stated as if she were reading my thoughts. "What, exactly would you not advise?" feeling my face turn slightly red. "Trying to jump out of a moving car is not a smart option, besides how bad could it be to spend some time with me, really?" giving me the most gorgeous smile I had ever seen, took my breath away, but only for a moment as the anger began to build again, "I had no intention of jumping from a moving car. Getting out at the next light, sure." Damn her, she had a way of making me say what I was thinking before I could even finish a thought. "Yeah, still not a good idea. How about you resign yourself to the fact that you will be spending a couple of hours with me and force yourself to enjoy the moment." she shot me that amazing smile again, I couldn't think. Why? Where? Shit, this was way past annoying. "Look I am sure you have lots of people who would love to have your company; unfortunately, I am not one of them. So be a good girl and let me out," I stated as though making fun of how young she was would get me what I wanted. "Really? How old do you think I am?" she seemed excessively amused with herself and the driver was all but laughing at this point. "What difference does it make, but I am thinking late 20's, early 30's. Unless of course, you are a plastic surgery nut?" I decided not to be nice. "Ouch, that hurt." She was genuinely laughing at this point. "Not even close, but thank you for the... um, compliment? I suppose if that is the best you can do, I will have to take it," she was grinning, finally, the laughter stopped. What was so funny? She cannot be more than 35 at the most, could she? Not a single wrinkle on her flawless face. Beautifully, kissable lips perfectly shaped, and thick eyelashes that stretched out towards the sun. Her skin so perfect, I would bet that it was as soft as it was supple. I caught myself reaching for her face, to caress it. I suddenly had this overwhelming urge to kiss her. I wanted to feel the heat of her tongue in my mouth. To explore the inside of her mouth with my tongue, suddenly I was smiling. "Not quite so unpleasant, the company I mean?" she was staring at me curiously. "At least when you are not talking." My smile faded away quickly, and the sarcasm was unmistakable. She continued to stare at me, until finally, she leaned into me, close enough that I could feel the warmth from her body and gentle air that passed between her lips as she spoke. I felt a tingling sensation between my thighs and squeezed to quiet the sensation. "Really, no talking? Then what would YOU rather be doing?" she planted her lips on mine with such force, I could feel my teeth cutting through my lip and the slight taste of blood. She lightened the pressure on my lips and started exploring my mouth with her tongue. She tasted so sweet like the nectar of the gods, and her lips so soft. I found myself wrapping my fingers in her hair, and my body moving closer to her, longing for her touch. I could feel her hands caressing my body, pausing at my breast, and lightly stroking my nipple through my shirt. The tingling sensation between my thighs was becoming unbearable and I squeezed my thighs tighter together to try to calm it. I felt her free hand slide effortlessly between my thighs and stroke the very site that was causing me discomfort. My breath caught in my throat and I froze. What was I doing? This was not right, she was extremely attractive physically, but her attitude was horrendous and unacceptable. My body was hearing none of this; it only became more alive and more excited with each stroke of her hand, on my breast and between my thighs. I was slowly coming to my senses and found myself striking her across the face with all my might; I was surprised that she only just looked at me curiously. "I wouldn't have pictured you as a fighter, someone who runs sure, but not a fighter. This could be interesting," the tone of her voice made the hairs on my neck stand up again. I am not sure why but, on some level, I feel as though I should be scared, the queasiness in the pit of my stomach was screaming at me. It was all I could do not to jump out of my skin, I felt as though there were a shift in the universe and my mortal soul was at stake. Ok, ok, now that was dramatic, I must get control of myself or I would soon need a straight jacket and a room with padded walls.

"I don't really give a shit what you think," unable to admit that I was crushed by her observation. "Now back off," I stated as angrily, with as much venom as I could muster. She sat there just looking at me, well looking through me if the truth be told. Nevertheless, I would not back down, who in the hell did she think she was? What made her so perfect that she could try to run my very existence? The more I thought about it the madder I became. Finally, when I felt as though I was going to explode, she stated quite simply, "You my dear are going to be my guest until I decide otherwise. You will be polite, at least to others we come in contact with and you WILL behave yourself." My mind was in a fog again, what the hell? "I don't think so,

I will not be your play toy to be treated however you see fit," I stated with indignation. "You are just some random person I had the misfortune to run into, I have no intention of prolonging my stay in your presence," now that should put her in her place, at least that is what I thought.

"Let me clear up a few things for you, my dear. First, you ARE going to be my guest, meaning that I will be as respectful of you as you are to me. As for how you will treat anyone outside the two of us, YOU WILL BEHAVE. I can promise you, you will NOT like the consequences of pissing me off. Secondly, you have no idea what I can and will do to you if you provoke me, believe me, there are much worse things I can do other than kill you," her face was void of emotion, but I could tell she was not bluffing. I had nothing to say, I just let what she had said sink in. Why would this beautifully gorgeous woman be concerned about keeping company with me? Who was she? Why did she feel it necessary to threaten me? What did she mean things much worse than killing me?

"Look I don't know what your deal is? Don't really care, but I am sure you can have the company of any man or woman that you want, why are you forcing me to tolerate you?" I asked venomously.

"As I recall you were very much into me yourself moments ago. I can see and feel the passion that you are locking up inside yourself and I intend to see it more closely. I find you remarkably interesting, alluring even. I can have anyone and usually do, even those that try to deny me" she cocked her head as she looked at me, as though I knew exactly what she meant.

"Look, I don't give a flying fuck what you want. Or

what you thought about my response to your maneuvers a few minutes ago. What I do want is to be as far from you as possible" I was practically screaming at this point. Her eyes grew dark and a smirk crossed her face. She grabbed my arm, hard and yanked me down flat onto the seat. "Let me give you a better idea of what you're up against here," she leaned over me with her body pressed hard into me, maneuvering my arms underneath me. Once she was sure, I could not move she lowered her full weight onto me, my breath caught in my chest and I felt like I couldn't breathe. With her other hand, she grabbed hold of my face, looked into my eyes and for the first time she bared her teeth. I noticed the fangs right away. I was mesmerized by the way she ran her tongue across her teeth, slowly and deliberately. "As I said there are much worse things than death," I felt her breathe on my neck, as her tongue traveled down my right jugular. It felt like I was on fire, my body arched upward towards hers, pressing us closer together. I felt a light pressure on my neck, not quite a bite. My pulse started racing faster and my breathing became erratic. I pressed my throat into her mouth, I had no control, I could feel myself moving but I could not stop. Her scent was intoxicating; my mouth was watering. She trailed her tongue down my neck to the crest between my breasts, ever so lightly I could feel her teeth as they grazed my skin, I felt the goosebumps rising all over my body. Suddenly the car came to a stop. I felt her grip loosen slightly, but only for a moment. Her grip was crippling. The door opened and she effortlessly scooped me up in her arms, carrying me inside. "Your services will not be needed for the rest of tonight, Harold." she laughed, and the driver joined in as though she had told a joke. She swung open the door, and then closing it swiftly behind her, he was gone. She never missed a beat, or a step for that matter. The room was dim, but even with little light, I could tell she had very expensive tastes. The room became a blur, I never felt us ascending the staircase. Before I knew it, I was being placed on an enormous bed, so soft and comfortable, the bed linens must have been made of silk for every time I moved I felt as though I was sliding on a pool of water. The air was cool. Suddenly, she was beside me again, her naked body lain out beside me. I found myself admiring her body, I never felt my own clothes being removed; it was as though I was drugged. I was helpless to move or do anything. I wanted only to be closer to her; my heart was beginning to ache. My chest was feeling heavier, I moved closer to her and as I did, the ache became less noticeable. My hand was moving across her body, starting at her neck, trailing down to her breasts, I made small circles over her nipples that became firm with my touch. My mouth teasing the hardened areola, as my tongue swirled effortlessly over it, with a slight sucking I could feel her quivering under my touch. I was consumed with desire for her; she filled my mind until nothing else existed. Our bodies were intertwined, caressing each other softly becoming more feverish with each touch.

I felt her fingers as they entered me, softly but urgently. Our lips never parted, as she skillfully brought me to orgasm. I had the profound feeling of ecstasy, but at the same time, an out of body experience like I was watching us from above. I saw my back arch and my fingers clawing the sheets beneath me and just when I felt I could take no more or surely go insane, I came again. It was like no other feeling I have had before. Slowly, rhythmically moving in and out of me. It was as though we were one, moving simultaneously together. Slowly she pulled herself from me, gently pulling her lips from mine and slid her tongue down me until she reached the softness between my thighs. I felt her tongue licking my clit slowly at first and then with more urgency, as her fingers entered me again. My breath caught in my throat, "OH, MY...." I was screaming in ecstasy, "more, more" I begged, as I showered her. My body was moving with each thrust of her hand, my back arching to get closer to her. Grabbing her shoulders, I pushed with all my strength, she was taken by surprise and I easily maneuvered her beneath me. I needed to feel her, to touch her, to be inside her. I saddled her body beneath me, slowly I entered her moistness. I choked back a cry of ecstasy, as I felt her rise to meet my fingers and felt the moisture of her sweetness. She moaned and arched into me, as I began to move my fingers inside her she, rocked back and forth with her hips. Moving slowly at first, then from beneath me I heard a faint whisper from her, "faster, faster." I did as she requested, with the passion rising inside of me. I was barely aware when she moaned, "OHHHHHHHH" her body going rigid for several seconds every muscle tightening, her breath catching in her throat and then releasing. We made love, with no sense of time or place, until we both fell fast asleep from exhaustion.

The morning came way too soon, with sprays of sunshine falling over us. The curtains for the most part kept the light from devouring us. There was just enough light that I could gaze upon her flawless body and bask in the beauty of her. Her skin glistened like that of a diamond. I was dumbfounded that someone of her beauty could want me and please me so completely. I longed for her to take me again. She rolled over and pulled me closer to her, I loved the scent of her. The light musky smell with a hint of cotton candy, that's what her scent reminds me of freshly made cotton candy. I smile to myself and inhale deeply savoring every moment.

She rises on one arm and stares into my eyes, a smile taking shape at the edges of her mouth. "I hope you understand, my pet. That now you belong to me. You have always belonged to me." She stated as a matter of fact. I was unsure of the look I saw in her eyes; I could say nothing. She leaned into my neck and for a second, I felt a sharp pain as her teeth pierced my skin, then I was falling into a dark nothingness, my head was becoming heavier and I could not move. Darkness....

Had I been dreaming, was any of it real? I was falling through the darkness, there was nothing to hold or grasp onto. I just kept falling. Thinking to myself, "damn it is really going to hurt when I finally land". Suddenly, I realized the truth in that statement. I didn't actually land; it was more the awareness of the pain that brought me back to my senses. My head was pounding, and my throat was throbbing, I grabbed my neck with my hand and felt the dampness. I pulled my hand back to look at it, and there was blood, my head became foggy and I fell back into the bed. I do not know how long I was out of it, but it must have been hours, for there was no longer sunshine peeking from behind the curtains, I could see a sky full of stars. Someone had opened the curtains on the huge windows (which must have been about 6-8 feet high). The room was amazing, with vaulted ceilings and rafters. There was an old feel to this room, the furniture looked antique and exquisite.

I thought I was alone in the room. I jumped from the bed and ran to the door, grabbing the doorknob, I realized quickly that it was locked. Suddenly, the events from last night came rushing back, the amazing sex and then the bite. "Oh, hell. What has happened to me?" I ran to the huge antique-looking mirror, "thank God, I still have a reflection." I stated while I was examining the two small puncture marks on my neck. "Nice. It amazes me how people actually believe the garbage they see on TV," a voice from somewhere in the dark. I was so taken aback that I swung around so quickly, I made myself dizzy. "What are you talking about?" I stated. She gently grabbed my arm and we stood there facing the mirror, our reflections looking back at us, mine was one of bewilderment, hers of amusement. I had to stop my mouth from falling open. "No, we don't lose our reflection, don't burn up in sunlight, although our skin is more sensitive to it and we cannot be killed by a wooden stake" no humor there. "Then what?" I was dumbfounded. "We require blood to survive; many choose to live off of animal blood. Most prefer human blood, like me." She smiled wide enough to show off her fangs. "We are stronger, have more stamina, but do not live forever." She was so mattered of fact. "Generally, we end up killing each other; we tend to be very territorial. We can live for hundreds, even thousands of years if left alone by others of our kind. But generally, we fight amongst ourselves for more space." She seemed to be talking at me and not too me at this point. "I am over 300 hundred years old; I was changed when I was 30 years old. Therefore I look like the perpetual 30-year-old. If humans were well maintained they would resemble us, but all the crap they put on and into their bodies it is no wonder they die at such young ages. We heal quickly from flesh wounds and are never plagued with illness or disease. I do not like to think about the early years, so I suggest you do not ask. I like this time and place much better at least in the last 20 or 30 years. We pass on a modest fortune to those we turn. They have the choice to stay with us or move on, and never cross paths again. If you know what I mean. We are not monsters; we do not devour our prey. There is no reason to gorge on human blood; it is of abundance to us. Thus, we do not have to kill the food, we take what we need to survive and move on. Those puncture marks on your neck will be gone in less than 24 hours. It's called being at the top of the food chain my dear." She must have noticed my grimace for she stated, "Don't be such a child, you eat meat, your kind consume large quantities of it. What you do not eat goes to waste. We only take what we need. Now that is not to say that on occasion one of us won't go overboard and kill someone, it has happened, thus the stories, but generally, NO. We just want to be left alone to enjoy life." She was so mattered of fact about the whole thing. As if, she was talking about how to bake a cake or explaining being a vegetarian. I was dumbfounded, and for a moment, I could not speak, then my mind swirled with all kinds of questions and fear started to set in. All the stories I had ever heard about vampires or all the movies, had all ended badly; even the good vampires were seen as bad. How could this be? This was not possible? Was this possible? Could there be a race of superhumans? Vampires? She is so beautiful. Over 200 hundred years old, she said she was over 200 years old. My mind refused to comprehend all this new information. IF she bit me would that make me a vampire? "No, you are not a vampire." She stated with some sarcasm. "I was not trying to turn you, just to have a little desert, as it were." She laughed. I was not finding any of this funny. I was getting tired of being a pawn in everyone else's game. "I want; therefore, I take. What the fuck kind of attitude is that? I am officially done with this business" I stated out loud, to my surprise. In less than two days, my life had changed from what I had known it to be. Everything I thought I had known was wrong. What else was there out there that I did not know about, the things that go bump in the night that really could kill you? Was there really a boogieman, and if so, is that really why young children went missing? Should I run, but to where? Would it even do any good to run? I knew her secret, does that mean she will have to kill me now. "I will not be killing you" she stated with mild annoyance clear in her voice. "Ok, how do you keep doing that? Can you read minds too?" I questioned. "I have lived for a long time; it doesn't take much to figure out what you're thinking. I cannot read your mind exactly, but I can get a glimpse of what you are thinking in your mind's eye." She stated simply. As a thought started to form in my head, I stopped it before it could be completed. "I am not sure whether I should be scared shitless or flattered that you feel my time is worth your attention." I stated drily.

She left the room, without another word, locking the door behind her.

Chapter Six

What now?

Katherine stormed out of the room, angry not with Ashley, but with herself. "This is not how it is supposed to be. I did not bring her here for this. I just wanted to get to know her." Katherine thoughts wondering back to Ashley. "I have loved this woman since the assault, watched over her. What was I thinking? How could I put her in danger now? Am I really that selfish?" Katherine headed downstairs, furious with herself.

Walking aimlessly around the house, Katherine was contemplating what to do next. Her thoughts were interrupted by Harold. "There are some things that need your immediate attention," he stated. "What is it? Has something else happened?" Katherine questioned. "There has been another murder by the newbies," he stated. Katherine looks up the stairs and thinks to herself, what have I done? Katherine follows Harold, listening as he explains the situation.

"What now? Why did she call me her pet? Am I supposed to be her love slave now? Love obviously had nothing to do with this. I do not fucking think so. She may be able to get me to do as she pleases when she pleases, but damn it I will make this as uncomfortable for her as I can when I am of my own free will" I swore to myself. "I have known some cold-hearted bitches in my time, well maybe not as long as she has, but none the less. Some really cold-hearted bitches, but she takes the cake." Dumbfounded, I sit down in the vanity chair and look at myself in the mirror. I have often sat looking at myself in the mirror, wondering how the hell I got myself in this situation. Well for the first time, I did nothing to cause this, but I do not feel any better. I should feel a sense of relief, that this time it is truly not, my choosing, but I do not. I have been plagued with poor choices all my life, now the one time I try to make the right choice, there is NO choice to be made. I am an unwilling participant in her game until she says that the game is over. I am now truly in HELL!!! It did not take long for the tears to start and even less time for me to fall into a series of terrible dreams. I did not know what to expect when I woke up, but I did not expect to be in bed at my cabin. I ran to the mirror, thinking I must have been having another episode of dreams. Maybe last night never happened? Looking into the mirror, I could see by the bite marks (that barely still lingered) that I was indeed not dreaming. Then how? I did not understand.

"No worries, My Pet" that voice, where was it coming from? "I am in the living room, just waiting for sleeping beauty to decide to finally wake up" noting the moderate amount of sarcasm in her voice. "I have some business to take care of, so I thought it best if we continue our adventure at a later date," she stated as a matter of fact. "I see no reason to continue anything," I stated. "Well, it is fortunate for both of us that I do. I will see you when my business is completed. Not to worry, everything I need to know about you, I do. So enjoy your family reunion. My Pet." She did not even wait for a response; she walked out the door and was gone.

What was I supposed to take from that? I was now her toy? She did say that now I belonged to her. I have news for her, I belonged to no one. Hell, not even myself. What now? That is all I could think of "what now?"

Finally, I have a moment to collect my thoughts. A moment without her constantly inside my head, trying to read my thoughts. What the hell have I fallen into and how do I get out of it? I do not have a clue about what I should do next. I just had the most incredible sexual experience in my life and with a vampire. Ok, now I know it is time for the rubber room with the straight jacket, and the people in the white coats to come to take me away. I am living this nightmare and I do not believe it. Think this through, she stated herself that they are not invincible, they can be killed. She had technically done me no harm, as of yet. Well, unless you count the damage to my pride. I hate that feeling when someone has so totally gotten under your skin and there is nothing you can do about it, no way to stop it.

Damage to my pride, what a joke. Did I even have any pride any longer? With each of the devastating relationships I have been in, I have lost not only pieces of myself, but my pride as well. Especially with this last one, I took her back so many times after she had done some despicable things. She had no regard for me or my feelings, and yet I took her back time and time again. Why? I am sure that a part of me loved her, but how could I expect her to have been any different the next time or time after that? She never changed nor did her behaviors. A truly selfish bitch, my only peace of mind comes from knowing that one day she will have to face what she has done. Another of my Grandmother's favorite sayings, "it is not up to us to make others pay for what they have done to us. For what goes around will eventually come around. You reap what you sow," she would say. Little constellation when you feel as though you have been thrown out like a piece of trash. I just want to know what the hell I did to deserve this? Nothing that I am aware of, once again did I live a treacherous life in my previous time here on earth and now I pay for it throughout my whole existence in this life?

I have lost my faith in the honesty of others. I no longer look for the good in anyone, for all I see is the bad. I have lost my ability to trust for now, every time I hear someone explaining something, I thought to myself; are they serious? Did it really happen? Or are they lying? I know that it is not possible that everyone in the world is a liar, but I cannot help but feel that way. How do I go about regaining my faith in people when they have shown no regard for anyone else? This is my dilemma; how can I stop being a hater and start to love again? And on top of all of this now, I have a psychotic woman calling me her pet, as though I am her toy. Why not I suppose, I have been a toy for others' pleasure before. At least this time, I may get some enjoyment out of it as well; I smiled at myself as my mind replayed the intense sex from the day before....

After being dropped off at the cabin I thought for certain she was just toying with me, and I would never see her again. I was wrong. Katherine came over the next day. "Hello, my Pet." She exclaimed from the living room. "Although, yesterday was very enjoyable and I would love nothing more than to have more of the same. How about we take the time to get to know one another?" Katherine stated simply. "Excuse me?" I stated with some confusion, and not knowing what else to say. I definitely wanted to know her. My body longed for her touch and my mind was out to lunch. "So, how about we go out on a proper outing?" she questioned. Even though it did not sound like a question, I sensed it was more like a fact, this is what we were going to do. "Let me get dressed. Where are we going? So, I know what to wear?" I stated as I knew I had no choice. I turned to look at her, her beautiful face was now mere inches from mine. I could feel her breath on my face. How I longed to kiss that face, to touch her lips....

"Let's do lunch and a hike, shall we?" Katherine suggested casually. I went to my room to change. Looking at my clothes, I wish I had brought more with me. But a t-shirt, cardigan and jeans would have to do. A little makeup could not hurt. Eye shadow, mascara and some lip gloss helped to settle my nerves a bit. What was I thinking? She is an arrogant and overbearing individual, but also gentle and caring, at least when she gets her way. I could see I was in for a heartbreak, but my brain was still out to lunch and my body was only thinking of yesterday. We went to Cades Cove for a picnic, she had everything for a lovely picnic: wine, cheeses, sandwiches and fruit. The lady came prepared. Then my mind started to wonder, do vampires eat? This should be interesting, I thought to myself.

"Tell me about yourself," I requested. "All I know is your name and that you are over 200 years old. Which is really blowing my mind." I stated with obvious curiosity. "What do you want to know?" Katherine asked. "Everything" I said. "Ok, I was born in a small town to wealthy parents. I had 6 siblings, 2 sisters and 4 brothers. We were extremely comfortable and traveled a lot with my parents. My parent, well my mother was into ministering the word of God to those that were underprivileged. How she must have turned over in her grave when I became a vampire. It was the time of the "black death", the plague, which killed without scrutiny. It did not matter if you were wealthy or poor, people were dying everywhere. We had over the years lost my siblings to various diseases and now we were dying, my father was in the worse way, my mother was not far behind and I well, I was fighting it as best I could. My uncle showed up and rescued me. My parents were too far gone. He saw all the death and knew that if he didn't act quickly, I would be next. So, he turned me. Giving me life."

She sat staring off into the distance, as though she was remembering what it was like then. I sat transfixed on her every word. Not knowing what to make of her story, a story she seemed so willing to share with me. I was awestruck. Why me? Why share all this with me? This woman had been through so much… "How old were you? 30, right? Still traveling with your parents?" I questioned. "Back then a woman in her 30's who was not married was considered a spinster and even though I had several suitors, I was not willing to settle. Besides in my young arrogance, I felt I was destined for so much more than a life of marriage and family. Being from a wealthy family, I was able to be well-educated. Even though it was frowned upon for women. I loved it when the tides turned, and women gained their rights. I went to an Ivy League school. I received my doctorate in social justice." She saw the look of puzzlement on my face and stated, "Remember I am the perpetual 30-year-old and have nothing but time, so getting my doctorate was just a drop in the well of time." Katherine stated.

"Your turn. Tell me about yourself." She requested. "Like what? I am not that interesting." I said. "Tell me why you don't like people or was that just me you didn't like?" Katherine asked. "No, I don't like people in general. They are too unpredictable." I said looking away. "What made you feel that way?" she questioned. "Well, a while ago I was shopping and when I returned to my car I was attacked. If it were not for a passerby I could have died. So ever since that day, my judgment of people has become jaded." I stated. "Do you remember much about the attack?" she questioned. "No, not really. I just remember waking up in the hospital after having brain surgery for a bleed that was caused by my fall from the attack." I looked away, tears filling my eyes. "I was there," Katherine stated, watching me closely for my reaction. "What?" I was stunned, did I just hear her say that she was there? "I saw the whole thing and nearly killed the bastard for hurting you." Her voice trailed off the anger unmistakable in her voice. "It was all I could do to keep from killing him. I remember seeing you across the parking lot and thinking what a lovely lady. Then this man from out of nowhere grabs your purse and punches you, you fell to the ground hitting your head on the bumper of a truck and then again on the asphalt. I could not just stand by, I grabbed him as he tried to leave and well let's just say he won't be stealing or assaulting anyone else again. I went back to you and stayed with you until right before you woke up in the hospital after surgery." Katherine turned her head away as though she was reliving a painful memory and I could tell she had tears in her eyes.

"I can't believe it; you saved my life." I was dumbfounded. I could not believe that she was the one. "I have been looking out for you ever since, call me your guardian angel," Katherine stated. "Why, why would you do that? You didn't even know me." I was in shock. Things were starting to come together; she was the figure I had seen on numerous occasions. She was watching over me. I was not sure what to make of her. "Ash, I have loved you for a long time now. I am sorry, how we met and how arrogant I was. I just needed to have a moment with you. To share how I feel. To bring some joy back into your life." Katherine was looking at me, searching my face, looking for some clue as to what I was thinking.

Oh my God, she has been the presence that has haunted me. I had turned my back to her. What do I do? What do I say? A part of me was scared and part of me was flattered. But the fear was making it difficult to think. What do I do? How could I just go on with the day like nothing had just happened? She was in essence stalking me. She was a part of my life and I had no idea. Ashley was becoming angry. How dare she take so many liberties with me. I could feel her move closer to me. Katherine placed her hand on my shoulder and turned me around. I looked her full in the face, with tears in my eyes. I looked at her. The feel of her hands on my shoulders sent shock waves through my body. Every neuron was alive with sensation. She pulled me closer to her, I could feel the heat from her body as she pressed up against me. My mind was not my own. I could not think.

She lowered her face to mine and gently kissed my lips. I was in shock and did nothing. She lifted her face from mine and looked into my eyes. My body was on fire, but the heat did nothing to melt the frozen part of me that was being taken over by fear. What did she want from me? What now? Why now? Ashley's mind was starting to come alive again.

Do I storm off angrily? Or do I accept the fact this amazing woman has chosen me to love and care for? How do I feel about this? Ashley's mind was racing, going over what happened back then, how things have been since the assault, and how things are now. This woman has just shared her secret with me. A secret about who she is and where she came from. She has confessed her love for me, and I stand here giving her nothing. I fell in love with her the first moment I laid eyes on her. My heart and body belong to her, she is the one. I see that now. The one that I have been waiting for.

"I am not sure how I feel about all that you have said. But one thing I know is that I love you too. I fell in love with you that day on the mountain. Call me crazy, but I feel as though I have been waiting for you all my life and all the lives I have lived up to this point." I confessed. Katherine was overtaken with emotion, she pulled me to her, wrapped her arms around her and kissed me. The most loving and gentle kiss, which I returned with the same loving gentleness. We stood like that for a while, just holding each other.

For days we could not get enough of each other. we spent every day together, loving each other, making love to each other and just being together learning about each other. It was as if time had just stopped and we were the only two people alive. We would lay for hours in each other's arms, just holding each other. Our bodies instinctively drew together and enter twined.

As we lay in each other's arms the phone rang. Katherine answered. "Hello." The voice on the other end, simply stated "it is time" and hung up. Getting up out of bed, Katherine told me, "I have some business to take care of, but I will be back, as soon as it is over." Then she bent over kissed me and was gone.

Chapter Seven

Taking Care of Business

How could this young woman have affected me so? I have lived for hundreds of years and no one has gotten this close to me. I feel as though I had done her an injustice if I do not turn her. She will be fighting for her life every day from enemies she has never known. Here I am going in for the kill and all I can think of is her, and making sure, she is safe.

"Ok, everyone should be familiar with the plan. Gordia, you go through the back with Mitchell. Trace and Lily through the sliding glass doors. Breck, Rachael and Wilma take a window. Chase and I will go in from the front. I have scoped out the current situation and there are currently three of the six newbies in the house. Shantini and her team are on the other three. Once inside, do not hesitate. Cut off the head. Try not to engage in hand to hand combat as they will be extraordinarily strong and agile, go for the head and do not miss. Once they are dead, we will set the house on fire and burn it to the ground, nothing but ash. Any questions?" Katherine stated without emotion. This definitely was not the time to be showing emotions. The girl was safe, back at the house. For now, no one knew of her existence.

These old deserted houses always were the first place of refuge for the newbies. Good thing too, no one around and no one to report a fire, at least not until the majority of the burning was done.

It is time, Chase and I make eye contact, on three: 1-2-3. Shattered glass and broken wood. Then came the screaming, as we attacked the first of the three newbies. The first was in the living room feasting on a fresh kill, he was so consumed by what he was doing he did not sense us coming, he went down with minimal resistance. The second was caught in the kitchen, a little more fight with this one, distraction was the key. Staying just out of reach enough not to get torn to pieces but provided enough of a distraction for my partner to cut off the head. The third newbie was in the bedroom. Simultaneously the heads were cut off. The body can be very fragile when someone takes a notion to cut your head off. The act itself was a work of art; everyone working at the same time to put down the mongrels that were threatening our way of life. We all had something to lose if even one of them survived.

Next, was the fire. A catalyst was used to give the fire the ability to consume and completely demolish the house, no chance for fire rescue to get here. Adrianna watched from a distance to warn if anyone was coming or to take care of any unforeseen visitors. She is also the one who was to stay behind and make sure the house was left in ashes. No evidence of us could be left behind. The subtle differences that occurred when we were changed would be enough to have police and doctors asking questions, we would not want answered.

My portion of the job was over, now I must check on the others to ensure that they were able to carry out their duties. I am a fine-tuned killing machine if that is what is required of me. I prefer not killing, I am not a barbarian. I do not enjoy the kill, the hunt yes, I enjoy the hunt. I do not relish in taking life, vampire or human. How is it that we are not the same? I was once human; I still believe in humanity. I still believe in good versus evil. To some, we are the evil. I take only what I need to survive, blood is not my only source of sustenance. I require many of the same comforts that humans need; I have many of the same wants as humans have. I am not human, but I am not unfeeling or uncaring either. I will not mourn over what happened here today, it is a case of the good of the many outweighs that of the few. Besides, it is the humanity that was taken from them that I mourn. They never had the opportunity to become anything more than killing machines; they were not taught or cared for. In this instance, it is just like putting down feral cats or rabid dogs. It is a necessity.

Shantini and her group have not checked in, it has been several hours past the check-in time. My team joins together again to locate the others in the event that newbies had gotten the upper hand. Deshali is concerned that he has not heard from any of the other team members. "Katherine, at some point we must assume that they are injured or dead," Deshali stated with great sadness in his voice. "I agree," stated Katherine. "It is time to finish this mess. Have we figured out who started this mess? Who is responsible?" Deshali takes in a deep breath, holds it for several seconds before exhaling. "It was …." He trails off, the sadness in his voice becoming unbearable. "It was Shantini, wasn't it? That is why she was so dead set on being part of the teams, to fix her mistake." I knew that this must be the case for Deshali could not bring himself to speak. Now she has paid the ultimate price, death: whether by the newbies or by us, there were no exceptions. Bending the rules for even one would cause chaos. It is by the rules we live by that keeps us in check. If there are no rules, then there are no boundaries that must be kept. Rules are like your word, in that if they do not exist then you are left with nothing.

Before I was reborn as a vampire, I had a family. I had a Mother whom I respected immensely. She raised me to hold one belief: there is truly only one thing that we own in life that is your word. If your word could not be counted on, then you had nothing. There are times in our lives when we truly have nothing, but if we are lucky, we find our way back before there is no turning back. This is one of those moments when there is NO turning back. I have known Shantini for most of my vampire life, I cannot imagine what happened to make her turn against a law that she helped to create.

I am disappointed that even after so many decades it is possible that you still do not know those that are closest to you. I would have bet my fortune that one of the outliers, those that wished chaos were our ruler, created the newbies. I would never have thought that Shantini was capable of such treachery, or stupidity, whichever was the case is of no concern to me now. The job has been done, at least for the three newbies that we destroyed and Shantini must pay the ultimate price for breaking the only laws that truly exist for us.

Shantini finally checked in six hours later than she was scheduled to. Four of her team had been killed. Shantini stated that they were lying in wait for them. Not only were they waiting for them, but there were several more there than just the three. She stated that the three that made it out alive were lucky. Lucky, because they did not sustain any life-threatening injuries from the encounter with the Newbies. It was as though they were meant to survive, meant to be a warning to anyone who tried to kill them. There was more crucial information to come, however, Shantini's voice began to crack and her body started to shake. Deshali walked over to her and placed a blanket around her shoulders and held her while she cried. Katherine stood in total confusion on her face. She stood waiting for Deshali to make his move and take Shantini out if he could not get the drop on her than it was to be me, Katherine thought solemnly to herself. Several moments passed and Katherine was getting anxious, she started to pace, getting closer and closer (like a lion stalking its prey). Deshali on the other hand had other plans. He knew that something was desperately wrong, for never in the last few decades had Shantini ever broken down like this....

Chapter Eight

Family Time

Unsure of what was going to happen next, I called my siblings and a few close friends to arrange for dinner. The restaurant is one of those buffet-style places. I get there early to ensure that we have enough space to accommodate everyone that is coming. The staff at the restaurant are helpful and pull several tables together for us. It is not long before people start showing up. My sister, Rachel and her new "supermodel" looking boyfriend showed up with the first round along with an old high school friend, her husband and 3 children (all boys). It is refreshing to see them all. Oh my, I cannot believe it. My brother is back with his ex-wife. Talk about dragging the sludge up from the bottom of the pond with that one. She took him for everything he had the first time, cannot imagine what she thinks she will get this time. She even slithers in like a snake, I wonder if there are people who are born part snake? At this point, if vampires exist, why can't snake people? I had to laugh to myself, how absurd. Wow, more people showing up all the time leave it to my family to invite everyone we have ever known.

"What's the matter, sis?" my bother Thad asked concerned. "What? Nothing." I said trying to sound convincing, should I tell him that I have been with a vampire (I think not unless I want to end up in a padded room with a white straight jacket). "Really?" he questions again. Guess I should tell him something because he won't let it go. "Just nervous about taking a vacation right now, since our company just went live on the new software," now that is something he would believe. "Yeah, I can see where that would be worrisome. But you have not had a vacation in a long time, and haven't seen your family in longer than that," he stated unsympathetically. Boy, leave it to him to point out the obvious and be blunt about. "I know, it was just never a good time," I stated simply. "Sis, you know I love you. But no one is around forever. We all love and miss you. Shit look how many people came to see you. You know, afraid you might kill over or something before you make another appearance," he stated seeming kind of pissed. He gave me a big hug and let it go.

"So how is everyone?" desperately needing to change the subject. That's all it took for everyone to get started and forget how long it had been between visits. The evening passed way too quickly. My brother Thad caught me on the way out, "I know there is more to this story than work, and I know you will tell me in your own time. I love you sis and I am just concerned," he hugged me again. "I know brother. One day I will tell you everything and more. You will think I am nuts, but what else is new?" We both laughed and made plans for the next few days as more people started to gather at my car to hear what the plans were.

The next morning, I arrived early at my brother Thad's place. "Yo, brother you up yet?" I yelled through the screen door; I knew someone was up I could smell the food cooking in the kitchen. The ex-wife was the one to answer and then the children came running to the door. "Yeah, you're here. Auntie come look at my room!!" All three of the girls yelled at once, grabbing me by the arms and pulling in separate directions. "Thad went to get more food, plates, and stuff. Once everyone heard you were coming, they decided to invite themselves," she stated somewhat annoyed. "Is Rachel coming?" that would be the sister with super-model looking boyfriend. "Not sure, I mean she will be here but not sure if HE will be with her," again with the annoyance. She was always such a hater. If she is not the center of attention, then she gets so pissy. Oh, well better to be pissed off than pissed on, I always say. A smirk crosses my face and I know that she did not miss it.

"Sis, glad you could make it. Be prepared there are already people parking outside. Hey, you still eat country food, right?" Thad said laughing. "Yeah, smart ass, I do." Laughing right along with him.

"Ok, girls. Show me your rooms, one at a time." I yelled from the kitchen. The girls came running, Sammie was first then Elsie, followed by little – Cammie. After getting a full rundown from each of the girls about their rooms and how they helped to paint and fix em up, we headed outside to see the rest of the place. Thad had done well for himself, a nice 2-story house on an acre of land in a quiet neighborhood. Quite the family man these days, hard to believe he used to be quite the player in the old days, cannot stop myself from smiling. Walking back inside I get a huge welcome from everyone I saw last night, but now the rest of their families are with them. Wow, I didn't realize there was that much room. Thad and Rachel had already started setting up tables and chairs outside on the deck, he had just built this past summer. He doesn't do anything small. The porch was almost the same square footage as the house but without the walls. Good thing it was so big or there would not have been enough room.

"I just wanted to say that I am glad that everyone was able to come. I know it has been a while, but you all were always in my thoughts, and in my heart," I could feel the tears welling up and turned my head. "Aww, shucks sister, you gonna make us all blush," Rachel was always the comedian, thank God for that.

It had been days since I had seen Katherine. I was beginning to think it was just a dream. Just as well as the next few days would be full of family outings and catching up. Now that I was home, I do not want to disappoint my family and being held captive by a vampire would definitely keep me from my commitments. The next several days were a blur: Dollywood, Gatlinburg, Cherokee North Carolina and a visit to everyone's home that came to dinner and breakfast.

Finally, a few moments to myself to collect my thoughts.... Maybe not such a good idea, same shit different day. What do you do when you are mind fucked on a daily basis? I damn sure do not know. But the events earlier in the week come flooding back again like they have every day since I first laid eyes on Katherine. The relationships of the past seemed but a distant memory for all I could think about was Katherine. She was amazing, not just because she was a beautiful woman (on the outside, anyway), but she had a sense of who she was and was not afraid to show it. I guess living for 300 hundred years has a way of doing that to someone, right? 300 hundred years, I could not even begin to understand the impact of all that time on someone. But damn she knew how to make love to someone.... I felt the discomfort between my thighs, she was telling me that it had been days since she had felt Katherine and she was not happy about that. Well, duh…. For the first time in my life, I find someone who can bring me to orgasm, not once but numerous times and then they disappear. Just like all the others. Oh shit, here I go again. Well, not really for low and behold who walked through the door? Katherine.

Chapter Nine

Clean up Time

I took my team and those that were left from Shantini's team and we went in search of the newbies, we found them celebrating their victory (short-lived as it was). They were so consumed in feasting on their dinner, they never showed any sign of hearing us coming. We split up and came in from all sides, with no hesitation and no mercy. Swords raised and heads came off until every last newbie was dead on the floor. The room looked like something out of some horror film with blood and bodies everywhere. This place was closer in and we knew that fire trucks would be here before it would burn completely so one by one stacked the bodies in a pile pouring gas on each one as we stacked, then threw gas around the room. The whole place may not go up in flames but this part would burn hopefully hot enough to destroy the bodies. Once the fire was set, we all scattered going our separate ways to meet up later, except Adrianne who was once again charged with watching the fire and reporting back. Instead of returning to my home, I went straight to Deshali to see if he had gotten anything further from Shantini. I found him sitting in his den. "Well, anything from her?" I questioned. Deshali nodded his head. "She is a broken woman. I have never seen her like this before. I know that she will snap out of it eventually, but we do not have the luxury of waiting." Deshali stood and walked around the room. He was pacing and that was not like him. He knew something, but I could tell by the look of him now was not the time to pressure him. "I don't think this is over, "he stated. "I know, we still have to deal with who made them," Katherine stated. "NO, I believe that there are more newbies than we knew about. I think there will be more murders." Deshali's voice broke as though he could not speak another word. "If there are more, we will deal with them, the same as the others," Katherine stated her anger starting to show. What was going on here, Katherine questioned in her mind. This is not like him, what is going on?

Chapter Ten

Meeting the Others

"Have you been keeping yourself busy, my pet?" Katherine's sweet sensuous voice trickles in from the living room. I felt her presence before she said the first word. "Don't call me that! I am not a pet, and definitely not to be toyed with," only a moment in her presence and the only emotion I wanted to feel was anger because I was hurt. I have missed her, but I refused to be treated as an object to be taken out and played with when she felt like it. "I apologize; I did not realize that is how you felt about being called my pet. I only meant it as a term of endearment," she smiled, but not the kind of smile one would expect if the apology were sincere. "Yeah, whatever. Why are you here? I haven't seen or heard from you in days. I thought you had finally come to your senses and moved on to your next toy," I stated with as much sarcasm as I could muster. Just being around her, I felt my anger slipping away. I had missed her; remembering that she could read my thoughts, I would never again allow a thought like that to form in my head for her pleasure or benefit. Katherine stepped out of the room, answering her cell phone.

Katherine was different tonight, as though something was weighing heavy on her mind. What the fuck, how would I know if this was different or the real her? I feel her inside my head, as though we are of one mind, one soul.

I cannot explain this feeling that has come over me. I can feel her presence before she is near me; it is as though I am looking through her eyes seeing what she is seeing only for a few moments we are connected. Then nothing, it all goes blank.

She is the one, the one I have been waiting for. A vampire. She makes me happy. I have been missing happiness for a long time. Shouldn't I be happy? Was this real? Could this really be happening? Is she the one? The one I have been waiting for through all of my past lives and now.

Katherine came back into the room, with a sullen look on her face, I approached her slowly. This was probably going to cause me more pain in the end, but I would rather it be my own decision than someone else making it or forcing it on me. I really did want to be with her; there was so much about her that I wanted to know. Also, I just wanted to be with her. I knew that I would end up just getting hurt, as that is how it always ended, but I wanted her so much more.

She gathered me up in her arms and held me there for the longest time, I did not move, I did not want to. I was incredibly happy to be in her arms, very safe and happy. I don't remember much about last night, just lying in her arms sobbing. Sobbing because I knew that I would be hurt again, sobbing for the innocence that I had already lost, and sobbing because I knew that losing her would be the end of me. I must have fallen asleep in her arms, for when I awoke, I was in the familiar surroundings of her home, in the bed we had … She was not beside me, nor was she in the room. Where had she gone? I rushed to the door, but it was locked. What the fuck, had we not gotten past locked doors? Did she not realize that she already had me in prison without any locks? Well, not a prison per say, but I was definitely not going anywhere. No, I wanted to be with her and had no intention of sneaking out like a thief in the night. She was like a drug, I needed her and wanted her...

There was a gentle knock on the door. "It's your house, only you can open the door." I shouted. I heard the key in the lock and the sound of it turning, "I am sorry ma'am I did not mean to disturb you, but Katherine told me to bring these things to you. She said you have 20 minutes to get ready and be downstairs." The young woman spoke very slowly and sadly. I could not bring myself to be mean to her. "Thank you, tell Katherine, I will be right down please," I told her smiling at her. "You don't have to be nice to me; I am just the hired help, ma'ma. Just kept around for sport and errands." She said apologetically. "I am so sorry that you are treated so badly." I could barely hold back the tears, is this what she had in mind for me? for if it were, she may as well kill me now. This poor child made to endure, what? Whatever it was, it must be horrible.

"Oh, ma'ma, no please you misunderstand me. I am well taken care of; it is just that sometimes Miss Katherine's guests can get a little out of hand and they like to play games with the humans. I am sorry, I have said too much. I must go." She pleaded, backing slowly out of the room. "Just call downstairs when you are ready, the phone is beside the bed."

I find it hard to believe that Katherine allowed her guests to get out of hand in her home, but I guess I am destined to find out tonight. The outfit that the young woman brought in was made of a silky type of material, made of royal blue and very elegant. Once I had finished dressing in the clothes that were provided, I opened the shoebox that accompanied the clothes. Inside were a pair of four inch heels that were the exact color of the clothes, with small jewels that accented the outline of the toe portion. I slid on the first shoe it was like putting on your favorite pair of sneakers (you know the old ones that are always so comfortable; they greet you like an old friend). I felt as though I was on fire with sensations that I had never felt before. My skin tingled, every time I moved the clothes seemed so fluid and such a part of me. These clothes and shoes must have cost a small fortune. How did she know my size? This was unbelievable. I opened my bag and from it, I took out the only makeup I ever used: eye shadow, eyeliner, mascara and some lip-gloss (caramel apple-flavored, my favorite smiling to myself).

I have quite the imagination, but never would I have imagined all this was possible. No one had ever made my body react the way she had, to move and moan the way she did. I was not prepared for the overwhelming sensations sweeping over me. I felt myself falling to the floor. Just before I hit, I felt arms surround me. "Like I said before, I can't even trust you to stay on your feet on solid ground. How have you survived life this long?" Katherine was back with a puzzled look on her face that turned into the most beautiful smile I had ever seen.

As Katherine and I descend the staircase, I can feel a great sense of accomplishment from the room below. There is such a feeling of immense satisfaction; I cannot explain it, these feelings that overcame me. As we reach the bottom of the staircase, we are approached by a very distinguished gentleman. Is he a vampire? It would be difficult to tell just by looking at him, but I had a sense that he was. "Hello, my dear. My name is Deshali, I am Katherine's Uncle", his voice was so soothing, almost like a lullaby. Then came a barrage of people introducing themselves. That portion of the evening was a blur, so many faces and names. I was surprised that there was a table full of food and an open bar. I was so hungry; I found my way to the food and tried a small amount of everything before the evening was over anyway. The feast was like an international smorgasbord, from appetizers to desserts.

Looking around the room, there were so many people here. Were they all vampires? I could not tell. I didn't allow my eyes to stay on any one person too long as I did not want to offend anyone. I glanced around the room making the occasional eye contact. People were for the most part, very friendly. I was not sure what to make of this situation. Was I the only human, except for the house help who by the look of the young woman who brought me my clothes was definitely human. I guess even vampires make chit chat. Deshali, I found to be the most interesting. He could maneuver a conversation seamlessly and he was definitely not boring. He shared about his recent travels to Egypt and the culture there; it was all very fascinating. I could have listened to him talk for hours. His voice was hypnotizing. He was pulled away by an older woman who seemed to want him to herself.

Not really wanting to get into a long conversation about myself, I steered clear of conversations that turned to me. I busied myself looking around the house. It was a very elegant blending of new and old. Some items looked incredibly old and expensive. I dare not touch anything for fear I would break it. I remember thinking: someone had exceptionally good, but expensive tastes. This was Katherine's home, what did it say about her? Did she have it decorated by someone else, or did she do it herself? How I longed to know more about her. As I found myself wondering and deep in thought, I barely noticed Katherine walking towards me.

"Come with me." Katherine stated without emotion. "What's wrong?" I questioned. She said nothing as she led me into what was obviously the library, so many books. "There is danger here, I need you to excuse yourself and request that Deshali escort you to a quieter location" there was a definite look of concern on Katherine's face as she spoke. "What is it?" I insisted. But she said nothing, it was clear that her mind was somewhere else; a feeling of dread was beginning to take hold of me. A feeling that I could not shake, it made my skin crawl. I did as I was instructed, I found Deshali in the corner of the room talking with a lovely young woman who seemed to be hanging onto his every word. I politely interrupted. "Deshali, if you do not mind could you escort me to a quieter room, as I fear I am getting a migraine." I asked as calmly as I could muster. "Oh, of course dear. Anything I can do to help." He was genuinely concerned, I could not imagine why a man of his years, stature and knowledge would care about a mere mortal like me. I began to have a feeling of calmness, a warm feeling overcame me. I had no idea why, but the feeling of dread had all but subsided. Deshali escorted me to a room that must have been a gallery of some sort. Wall to wall pictures of beauty; landscapes, portraits, statues, and other types of artwork were everywhere. "This is one of my favorite rooms in Katherine's home. She is quite the lover of art and knowledge" he stated with much pride in his voice. "Katherine is a woman of many convictions and very complicated" he continued to speak of Katherine as though she was one of his children and the pride in his voice was unmistakable. "She is definitely a force to behold" I stated with a half grin on my face. Deshali must have found this amusing for he burst out laughing. "I am sorry, did I say something amusing?" I was confused. The sudden laughter both interested me and scared me. "Katherine has always been a force to deal with, even before she became a vampire" he seemed to be reminiscing about a past long ago forgotten. "I have known her for a very long time" he was speaking, but not so much to me as to himself. "I have never known another like her nor am I likely to." He continued: "When Katherine was a child, her family was very wealthy. She was used to getting what she wanted and when she wanted. I had come into her world as her uncle. My family had long since moved away generations before her family even existed. My father and her great-great-great grandfather were brothers. I had married her father's sister. No, she was not a vampire, but she knew I was." His voice became extremely low and I noticed a tremor as he recalled these past events. "My wife was a uniquely beautiful woman, inside and out. I had matured a lot as a vampire over the hundreds of years prior to our meeting. From the first moment I laid eyes on her, I fell in love. She died during childbirth. Our son, he too died, but much later." His eyes welled up with tears, as he turned his back to me. "Katherine was but a mere child. She had only just begun to see the real world, and from all accounts, she was not impressed" He paused for a moment. "Several of her siblings died of smallpox and other diseases that year; she survived because she was away visiting with relatives in New York. She was not a sickly child, but during this time she had several close calls with death. It is unfortunate that her brothers and sisters did not make it. She was left an only child. Over the years, Katherine learned things very quickly picking up information and details that others missed. Even though her family had money, they did not live as most of the other wealthy people did, they lived very modestly. In her 30's she lived through the industrial revolution traveling abroad with her mother and her father who worked endless days to keep the family business afloat. While her father was working, her mother and herself assisted the area Missionaries assisting the locals. During this time in Prussia, the "Black Death" killed thousands; she too would have died, if I had not gotten there. I had planned to meet up with the family during my travels abroad. I was in Bavaria when I heard about the mass deaths from the plague in Prussia. I barely made it to her in time. I turned her immediately. I did not even offer her the option; I was selfish, as she was the sunshine in my otherwise dark life since losing my wife and child. I could not bear to lose her as well. She lost the rest of her family to the "Black Death"; I could not save them. Her father was the first to die just before I arrived. Her mother was in the latent stages of dying when I reached them. Katherine was in poor health, but she was a fighter, like none I had ever seen before, she wanted to live.

I had lived with the guilt for many years because of what I had not done. I lost my love, my wife, and my best friend. Then I was to lose our son. He and I shared a love of science and learning, but after that, science held little wonder for me, as I could not save the only one who made a difference in my life after my wife passed. She would not allow me to change her and made me swear not to change our son if he came out normal." "You mean human?" I asked with wonder, as I was wrapped up in his story picturing what it must have been like back then. "Yes, human. He was human and that frailty killed him but I had sworn to her, thus I lost them both." His voice trailed away and there was nothing more said. I wanted to ask him questions, to find out more about Katherine and his dead son, but I knew his pain and I dare not open that wound any deeper.

Time passed in silence; I had fallen asleep on the sofa. I did not know what time it was, or if anyone was still with me in the room, as it was so dark. I felt safe, even knowing that I was in a house with vampires I did not feel fear. Deshali's stories stuck with me, even in my dreams. Light shone through as someone opened the door and walked into the room. I stayed where I was keeping quiet. I had a sudden feeling of panic. I had no idea why, but my heart fell to the floor. I remained still and tried not to breath. Whoever this person was, he or she had no idea that I was here. The panic rose into my throat, I wanted to scream but dare not. "Ashley? Ashley are you there?" It was Katherine sounding concerned, almost overly concerned. "I am here, on the couch." I forced myself not to run into her arms. What was wrong? This cannot be good. I did not feel her or sense her. My mind was working overtime for all the possibilities, but nothing. My mind was blank except for the thought of her. I felt her take a seat beside me; I could feel the electricity vibrating from her. I had never experienced her like this. "Ash, you have to go. I will have my driver take you home. You must speak to no one. Tell no one of what you know or what you have seen." She moved closer to me and pulled me into her. I felt so safe within her arms. I started to ask her some questions, but she placed a finger over my lips, "I don't have time to explain, but your life may well be in danger." She sounded remorseful for the first time since I had met her. "Continue on your vacation as though nothing has happened. I will come to you when it is safe for you." She leaned into me and kissed my forehead.

"I don't understand but I will do as you ask." I felt a shift in this strange relationship that we have formed. I knew I must indeed see her again. She must be safe as well. I would say nothing, not mention anything to anyone. I would be alone again, but I knew she cared. I could feel how much she genuinely cared for me. I did not know why, but I felt as though we had finally found each other after a long separation that we were meant to share our lives together or was it just wishful thinking on my part.

"Come now, we must go." She grasped my hand and led me to another door. I never noticed this door before, but it must have always been there. "Follow this hallway until you get to the fork, stay to the left. Do you hear me? Stay to the left" she sounded almost panicked. "I will," I promised. I went through the door a soft light shown down the hallway. I felt her hand grab me, she pulled me into her and kissed me full on the lips and then she was gone. I continued down the hallway, it was damp and a little cold. It didn't take long for me to reach the fork; I stayed to the left as I was instructed. But the noise I heard coming from the right-sided hallway scared the crap out of me. Someone was screaming, I could barely hear them. But the sound stopped me in my tracks. I waited to make sure that the noise was not approaching me. I waited, being very quiet. The screaming suddenly stopped, I felt as though gravity had just become a force pulling me to the ground. I caught myself against the wall, just before my knees buckled from under me.

Chapter Eleven

The Next Assault

"Katherine, there is a problem." An older vampire approached from across the room. "What is it?" Katherine questioned. "We were wrong; there were more newbies than we thought. There have been some savage slayings in downtown, just about an hour ago." He stated with great concern in his voice. "How can that be possible? Unless they turned others? But how could they know how? They are too new to know how to stop themselves from killing; only with guidance do they learn." Katherine was shocked at the thought that there were more. The plan went off without any difficulty. How was it possible? A thought began to form in her mind, she shook it away. "Get Deshali! But be quiet about it." She stated with such force, her anger could not be disguised. There is no way there could have been more made so quickly. Shantini said there was more but we couldn't get much out of her, now she is in a safe house being guarded by Deshali's people. How do we know that she did not make them, damn it Deshali. His judgment when it comes to her is lacking. Unless, unless she is not the one who made them in the first place. Why would she take the blame for someone else, who would she be willing to take the blame for? This is cause for great concern; Katherine was running through the options in her mind. No, damn it no. I should have guessed it, I should have known. Shantini was too quick to step up and claim her guilt, how could I …. No wonder Deshali took her away before anyone else heard her rantings.

This problem must be dealt with. "What is it Katherine?" Deshali was at her side in mere seconds. Katherine explained what had transpired and laid out a detailed plan to correct the current situation. This time only core members of the Council would be involved in taking care of business. Deshali himself would lead one group and Katherine the other group. "I have to get Ashley out of here. I don't know how much has been overlooked but I do not want her to be harmed." Katherine was talking more to herself than anyone else. Ashley, what a beautiful woman, I have waited so long to have her in my life. I will not lose her now, not like this. I must get her out of here and to safety. Only those here tonight will know about her, no one else could possibly know of her existence or her importance to me. I will have Harold drive her to safety and keep an eye on her while I am away. Harold, one of my most trusted companions, he was family. I saved him years ago from being beaten to a pulp by his miserable father. That is one man who will never be found. Harold was tormented until he was 15 years old by that drunken piece of shit. Focus! Damn it! Focus! I know I can trust him. He is my son; no one knows what she means to me, but him. I will not allow anyone to use those I love as a weapon against me. I would sooner kill them myself as to have them tortured or worse….

Picking up her cell phone, Katherine called Harold. "Harold go to the east side entrance and wait for Ashley. I will send her out through the bowels of the house. Once she arrives, take her to her place and stay on her, of course without her knowing! There is going to be a war, and I want you and her as far from the fall out as possible. Take her to the airport and send her home to Florida. Yeah, that is a better idea. I knew I could count on you. Take the jet, that way you will arrive before she does. Take care." This was going to get nasty, especially if Shariffi (Shantini's brother) was involved. He is the only one that Shantini would take the blame for. She should have known better. He is a bad egg. Straight from hell, that one.

"Deshali, I have no way to be certain how many he has made at this point. We could be walking into an ambush." Katherine was finally relaying vital information about the true seriousness of the situation. "What do you mean? Who?" Deshali was confused, but only for a moment. "Shantini would have given her life for that piece of shit. What was she thinking? Brother or no brother, the law is the law. She was only delaying the inevitable." Deshali was enraged. There was no mistaking his demeanor. Shantini was his oldest and dearest friend; she was with him when he lost his wife and child. "I will kill that miserable excuse of existence myself."

"We must keep emotions out of it, do not underestimate him. He is very resourceful. There is no way he could have kept this so well hidden unless he had help. So now, we must weed out the conspirators. Which also means that there is someone on the Council who is aiding him? That person must have been the one to have gotten to Shantini. All of his miserable clan will go down with him this time." Katherine vowed.

The Council was called for an emergency meeting, in the Grand Room at Katherine's home. Many had to be located, but the meeting would be taking place tonight. The party was over, many had already left; the remainder of people began to feel a dread fill the house. [M1]Everyone gathered their things and hurried away not wanting to be in the middle of whatever was coming. The gloom made its way throughout the house, every room filled with un-ease and suspicion. The staff left the common areas; they knew that it was time to hide. They were mere humans; with no special strength or talents that would assist them in fighting for their lives should it come to that. Katherine had long ago made preparations for times like these. There was a vault in the lower bowels of the house that was self-sustained and secure. Once they were locked in, no one could get to them. It was Mr. Hobbit the head of the staff was in charge of making sure that everyone was accounted for, that no one was to be left out in the open. Mr. Hobbit took his job very seriously, and no one ever crossed him. He was the oldest of Katherine's staff and the most loyal.

"Now that everyone has finally arrived, it is time to initiate Code Red. It has come to our attention that not all the newbies were destroyed, or that there have been new ones made. Either way, we must find the source and extinguish it." Katherine was just getting started when a voice from the far end of the room spoke up. "I thought that Shantini had taken care of the last one's and that the situation was under control. Now you say that there are more, how can this be?" Emory a vampire of only 50 years had a way of stating the obvious. "It is true that every-one thought the danger was over. But now there has been a slaughter downtown, no mistaking what caused it. We must strike now to inhibit any citywide panic. Tonight, we take out the newbies and attack Shariffi. He is the one who started this." Katherine was setting out the plan when Emory piped up again. "How are we to fight Shariffi? He is strong in numbers and his place is a fortress. He has been a problem for many centuries and was left alone because of the truce between him and Shantini. Now you say we must take him out. Now that he is so powerful. What proof do you have? I will not be a part of this. Should you all fail, he will take his revenge out on the rest of us." Emory was speaking a truth that was all too real. Shariffi was not the forgiving type. His own sister had been ready to give her life to spare his. I am sure that she had gone to him and he knew what she would do to protect him. He would have let her die. He was dangerous, alright. More so than anyone could possibly imagine, what they did not realize however was that his plan was not to coexist with us or any other vampires, but to be the only vampire left.

Chapter Twelve

Protecting Ashley

Harold the driver was waiting at the exit of the tunnel holding the door open and gesturing for her to get inside. Jumping into the car seat I ask; "What's happening? I don't understand." Before I could even put my seat belt on, we were off. I could hear myself yelling, but the driver does not answer, he continues to calmly drive at speeds in excess of 100mph. My stomach starts to churn. What if he loses control of the car? What if someone pulls out in front of us, he would not be able to stop or swerve to miss them. I can hear a deep chuckle escape him. Damn, I keep forgetting some of them can read minds. I was very careful at the party, thinking random thoughts and hiding my surprise at how many vampires there were. I cannot fathom the actual numbers that must exist, the mansion was packed, wall to wall vampires and humans. Another chuckle, he must find this amusing. "Not really," he stated. "It's just that I have never been able to read someone so easy and I can't get you out of my head!" he laughed and so did I. He was a remarkably gentleman with old-world manors. "Tell me about you and Katherine please to take my mind off the current situation," I requested, shyly. "There is NO situation Miss," he lied and we both knew it," well I suppose there is no harm in it?" he chuckled again. He had a very relaxing way about him.

"Katherine and I met about…. 75 years ago, before I was turned" he became very quiet for a moment as though he was visualizing the event in his mind. "I don't recall much about my previous life, one of the perks, I guess. I vaguely remember being in a hospital. My father had beaten me so badly that he had lacerated my spleen and broke numerous ribs and other bones. That was the last night I ever saw him. Later that same night a woman entered my room, said she would save me from my tortured life. That was the first time I met Katherine. She became my foster mom and later she adopted me. She did just what she said she would do and took me away from my tortured life. About ten years later, there was an accident and I thought Katherine had died, even though they never found a body. Then when I was in the hospital again, dying of cancer this time, Katherine showed up again. I asked her if she was my angel come to take me home. She said no that she was there to give me life again. I asked if I would be able to see her again, she said "of course my son, I have always been with you and will always be with you". I remember the agonizing pain racking through my body as if it had been yesterday. I begged for her to help, anything just to stop the pain," His voice grew quieter and he paused. "She leaned in close to my neck and I felt some pressure, then immense pain. At that point, I must have passed out for the next thing I remember is waking up in the morgue. That is where I met my wife," he looked in the mirror and could see the surprise on my face. "Yes, we have been together for 55 years. She is as beautiful as the first time I laid eyes upon her. The bag was closed. I remember feeling panicked clawing at the plastic. I heard the most beautifully soothing voice singing "you get a line; I'll get a pole honey "…. It was like I was in a trance. I felt a tugging at the plastic as she unzipped it, "Hello, there handsome, time to wake up and start your new life." From that moment on, we knew we were meant for each other, even when I would close my eyes, I could still see her face. She took me to a place in the country; it was there that I saw Katherine, mother again. I had not seen her for 15 days; she raised me after my dad went missing. When I went away to college, I received a notice that my mother Katherine had died and left me some money in her will along with a note should anything ever happen to her. I never dreamed I would see her again, especially not on my death bed. Then there she was, alive and in front of me. Looking exactly as I remembered her. Katherine was very direct about her role in my future; she stated that she would teach me how to control the thirst, for if I did not learn control then she would also be my executioner, and no longer my teacher. I never doubted her for a moment."

All at once, I saw panic in his eyes. "No matter what happens, do not leave this car," he ordered, I nodded. The car was swerving, I could not see a thing outside of the car and we were going so fast. I could not even tell where we were, everything was a blur. Harold was cursing under his breath. If it weren't for his cursing or his white knuckles on the stirring wheel, I could not have known anything was wrong. His body appeared relaxed except for his hands and the smile he carried never left his face. He would be one hell of an opponent at poker, I thought to myself. The car jerked from side to side slowed only slightly then resumed its previous pace. The driver's smile widened and his grip relaxed "see nothing to worry about he stated with satisfaction in his voice; pleased with his own performance. I must have been holding my breath for I let out a huge sigh "AAAAhh" The moment was very short-lived as something slammed into the car; I knew I was going to die. Everything was upside down. I soon realized that the car must be rolling. Almost as soon as it started, it was over and my mind started to go black. "No matter what do not get out of this car!" Harold shouted at me, as the darkness was taking over my mind.

.... What is this place? There was no light, no sound, and no movement except mine and yet I was scared. I felt as though something horrible was going to happen. From the darkness came the sound of someone breathing, "Hello? Anyone there? Hello?" I started off asking quietly and slowly my voice rose, as no one answered. "Hello is ANYONE THERE?!" Nothing, nothing but the sound of breathing. Is it me? Is that my breathing? I tried to count my own breathes, but I was having to make a great effort not to hyperventilate and the sound was calm and rhythmic, almost hypnotizing. I suddenly felt a presence much closer now. "Hello, anyone there?" again no answer. Suddenly I felt a light grip of ice-cold hands on my arms, my breath caught in my throat as I tried to scream....

"Ashley, are you okay?" Katherine was leaning over me. I tried to move and fell into her arms. "I am now!" relief swept over me and I collapsed again. "What happened Ash, are you okay?" Katherine demanded. "She will be fine. We were making good time when I sensed a large group of Vampires coming upon us, at a remarkably high rate of speed. They had to be relatively new for their speed was unbelievable. At one point they shook the car, while it was moving."

"It seems as though we have underestimated our adversary," Katherine stated through clinched teeth. "Harold did you actually see any of them?" Katherine questioned.

"No, at this point I couldn't even guess how many there might have been." The realization of how quickly the event began and ended was mind-boggling. I was so glad to see that Katherine was not harmed; they must have thought she was in the car that had to be why they attacked. At that moment, I raised my eyes to Katherine and immediately knew that was not the case. They were after me? Katherine nodded her head in agreement. But why? What had I done to them or anyone? Katherine had a sad look about her eyes that tugged at my heart. "Was it because of my relationship with you?" Again, she nodded. "Harold it is time to step things up. The plan is no longer to return Ash to Florida. You and Sara will escort her to the safe house; if I find or sense that any portion of the plan has been compromised, I will contact you with the Satellite phone. Katherine was continuing with plans to keep me safe, sending two of his most trusted allies away to babysit me. "Absolutely, not!" I screamed. Katherine and Harold continued as though I had said nothing. "I know you both hear me, I will not be a liability to you, any of you," I stated. "Ash this is not the time," Katherine wearily stated, with as much conviction as she could muster. I took her by the hand and gestured to Harold to wait a few moments. "We do not have time for discussion, My Darling. I must get you to safety," Katherine sounded for the first time since we met unsure and afraid. "A vampire afraid?" I questioned. "Only for your safety." Katherine was overwhelmed with emotion and for the first time in what I am sure has been centuries, she wept. I wrapped my arms around her, holding her, whispering my love for her. Anger welled up from deep inside of me. Katherine looked up shocked and confused; for once, I could read her mind. "No, my love. I could never be angry with you again," I smiled, and she relaxed slightly. Her eyes registered immediate understanding, "Ash do not even think about it, I will not allow you to be put in harm's way. I have spent years watching over you, loving you. I will not allow anything to happen to you, not now. Not ever." She was panicked. Her eyes widened; a look of madness flashed across her face. "No, I will not do it!" Now I was confused. "Do what?" I asked. "Harold seems to think I should turn you. Turn you into one of us, so that you can defend yourself." I was confused but only for a moment, "No, that is not an option." I turned to Harold, "I appreciate your concern, but if it is my time to go then today is a good day to die." I stated plainly. Both of them looked at me with surprise. "I have never wanted to live forever, the mere fact that I lived this long often burdens me." Confusion still showed on both of their faces. "I don't want to die by no means. But I also do not want to live forever. I am a practical person. I would never want to outlive my friends and family. I understand that you have seen many things and have lived numerous lives, but I have no desire to." With that, I turned and walked away.

Katherine followed, and I approached the subject from a different angle "I know you would never allow any harm to come to me, of this I have no doubt. But what you must understand is that I cannot allow your emotions for me to cloud your judgment. This is not about you or me. This is about the survival of our people. There is someone out there plotting against vampires and humans alike. No rhythm or reason, just murderous indifference. You and your kind are all that stands between them and the certain death of humanity." I stopped, but only for a moment, to be sure I had Katherine's full attention. "You are vulnerable as long as you are protecting me." The puzzled look on Katherine's face showed that more of an explanation was needed. "I look at life and death differently than most people. Do not get me wrong I do not have a death wish, nor would I ever end my own life. However, one thing I have learned is this: Life is terminal; from the moment we are born, we know that we are going to die. No one knows how much time they have. We just make the most out of the time we have. You were given a rare gift, one that keeps death from your door. A precious opportunity to live out an exceptionally long life and accomplish those things that most never will. You and those who follow the rules keep a fine balance between our worlds, but now someone wants to destroy that balance. No human can know how to kill you, otherwise fear would cause us to turn on your kind and kill them all. Fear is a strong motivation. Therefore, you and your people are all we have to keep that balance. There is no other option. You and your friends, all of your friends must go and fight as there is no room for failure. Now that I know how they track me; I will keep my thoughts random and stay on the road stopping only long enough to take care of the essentials. I will require a car, a cell phone, and a large amount of cash. I will check in with you often, but you must go." Katherine was stunned, how could she possibly take care of herself. Hell, she can't even cross the street without practically getting run over. I know she is right, but how can I leave her unprotected, if they catch her, she would wish that death is all they wanted. The fact that she is alive after that attack shows me that they have other plans for her, and there are far worse things than death. "Katherine, please." I begged while fighting back the tears. "It is up to you to protect the people of the world from absolute desolation. There is no reasoning with them, you said so yourself. They were never taught to fight the lust for blood. No matter how much they take, they want more and more, the "blood lust" consumes them."

Katherine knew I was right but how could she leave me unprotected and alone. "I will go with her" Sarah stepped out the shadow where she had been talking with Harold. "Take Harold and go. We will be fine. We will keep moving until you tell us that it is safe to stop. Like Ashley said, we will only stop for the essentials." Sarah met Ashley's eyes without even a blink. "No, you must help Katherine." I stated breathlessly feeling as though the wind had been knocked out of me. "Katherine will not leave you alone. I am a good fighter, but my best skill is diversion and illusions. Together we will remain in the shadows. Together we will survive." Sarah seemed so confident. "OK, as long as you agree to allow Sarah to escort you, I will go and eliminate this problem." Katherine sounded determined and angry. "I know this is for the best, but if anything happens to Ash, they will all pay," Katherine stated and walked away.

"Thanks for your help Sarah," I said casually as they were walking towards the car. "No point in arguing with her. She would never have given in, anyway. Not with you on your own." Sarah's sweet lips turned up in a makeshift grin. I noted the insincerity in that statement and without letting my mind dwell on it, I decided to keep a close eye on Sarah, something was not right there. She was not as Harold had described, not at all. Sara had olive skin tone, dark hair (almost black), and grey eyes (quite startling at first glance). But it was not her eyes that were concerning, it was her mannerism. It appeared so forced, it was as if she had to think and then act, every movement was deliberate, from the way she walked to how she pronounced each syllable of every word. I could not quite put my finger on it.

"Ashley, I know we just met, and it is asking a lot, but you are going to have to trust me. When I tell you to move, move. A moment's hesitation could cost you your life." Sarah's voice was soft but well controlled. I just nodded my head, yes seems to be the way with vampires, to follow orders blindly at least when they are barking them at me. I am not so sure of Sarah; I will just have to trust Katherine and Harold's judgment for now.

I am glad I said my goodbyes to my family already; at least for now, no one will miss me until my co-workers realize that I am not back from vacation in two days. I could feel the life drain out of me, but at the same time, I felt exhilarated something about the unknown that excited me.

Chapter Thirteen

Finding the Trail

Katherine and Harold were headed to Deshali's home. The satellite phone was given to me (of course). The one attempt to reach Deshali by phone failed, could the newbies have mastered the ability to coordinate an all-out attack on the clan? Was the attack on Ashley a mere diversion to take out our leader? NO! I cannot look at it like that; Katherine reprimanded herself for even thinking such a thing. Deshali had been around for centuries he had talents no one knew about. It would be next to impossible to get the drop on him. An uneasy feeling was creeping up from deep inside, but she refused to give in to fear, that would help no one. The drive took just over an hour. Pulling into the driveway, Katherine had a strange feeling, all the lights are out, Deshali never allowed all the lights to be turned off. He always reasoned that what if a wayward traveler happened upon the house the darkness would have been unwelcoming, Katherine was thinking to herself. "Cut the lights Harold." Katherine's voice became quiet. Harold obeyed and turned the lights off, as they made their way slowly down the driveway. Harold and Katherine were on high alert, their senses screaming something bad had happened here. There was no movement inside the house or outside for that matter. "Maybe Deshali forgot to pay the electric bill." Harold thought, Katherine shot him a scornful look. Parking the car away from the house was a mundane concept for if it were vampires, they would have heard us a mile away, especially Newbies, as all their senses were heightened. They grabbed the weapons from the backseat and preceded slowly inside, the door was ajar. "This is really not a good sign" Katherine noted. The house was pitch black and just as silent. They separated at the staircase, Harold going up the stairs to check it out and Katherine checking on the downstairs. Harold was out of sight in seconds upon ascending the staircase. Slowly Katherine made her way from room to room. Where were Deshali, and his staff? No bodies, no smell of blood or decay. This was truly troubling. Finishing up in the kitchen the lower portion of the house was clear. Within minutes Harold was back, the upstairs was clear as well. They looked at each other, dumbfounded. "What the hell?" they stated simultaneously. At that moment, the phone rang, "Hello?" Katherine was the one to answer. "Katherine is that you?" it was Deshali, he sounded confused. "Where is Ester? I told her to stay by the phone," he responded. "There is no one here. The house is dark and deserted." Katherine replied with notable annoyance. "What? No one is there? That is impossible!" Deshali sounded confused and angered. "Ester was to have some associates over; she said they shouldn't be more than a couple of hours for them to iron out their differences. I asked if there was anything I could do and she practically threw me out of the house, stating that she would ensure that there was no mess for me to deal with when I came home." Katherine interrupted, "Who were these associates she spoke of?" Deshali stated he was not sure, he never questioned Ester. Ester has been with him for centuries, or so it seemed. "Other than you, she is the only other person I would trust with my life," Deshali stated with much conviction.

"I am on my way home now; I will be there in a few minutes. Stay and wait for me," with that Deshali hung up the phone. "What happened here?" Katherine was very puzzled by the latest turn of events. The newbies attempted to attack Ashley, now Ester is missing. How could this be? Newbies have never been known to have such control, to be able to plan and carry out something like this. What am I missing? Katherine was never one for second-guessing; she had an intuition that has served her well over the years. Ok, what do I know? Katherine was asking herself. Harold returned from searching the parameters of the property and the outlaying buildings. "There was nothing unusual that jumped out at me," Harold stated with a perplexed look on his face. "I don't understand what is happening here?" Harold stated with some level of annoyance. "Nor do I," Katherine followed. "How is it that the newbies are so organized? Unless they are not newbies at all unless they are. ...." A noise from outside interrupted Katherine thoughts, she and Harold went outside to investigate, poised for a fight they quietly but quickly walked outside. "Damn this old car, I couldn't sneak up on anyone in this damn thing," Ester yelled. "Ester, where the hell have you been and why would you need to sneak up on anyone?" Katherine asked with some confusion. "I wasn't talking about now. I was attempting to get some information on all this insanity, but my contact did not show up, so I went in search of her. Just as I pulled up in front of one of her hangouts, this damn car decides to backfire. What the f...? I threw the car in park and ran inside; I was too late. Everyone inside was dead or dying, a real slaughterhouse. I did get an interesting piece of information from one of the dying; he said that there are no newbies. He also said that there was a mole, Sarah. Harold's Sarah. But she is not the real Sarah. I don't understand, how can all of this be?" Ester's confusion was obvious; she wandered away talking to herself. Katherine froze. How could that not be Sarah? What is going on here? I have to get to Ashley, but I cannot leave now. Harold, I will send Harold. A few moments later Deshali showed up. "Where is Ester?" he seemed almost overwhelmed with concern for his old friend. "I am right here, why are you yelling?" she was getting agitated. "What happened to you tonight? You know you never leave the house without an escort, especially now." Deshali was practically yelling at her. "You ain't my Daddy or Momma, now lower your voice and speak to me appropriately." She had no problems standing her ground, she reminded Katherine of Ashley (a much older version, of course, she smiled to herself), the smile slowly faded as the current situation came flooding in. My sweet Ash, she is in such danger and has no idea of what she is up against....

Ester speaks up, "hmm, you with us Katherine? I was asking Deshali how is it possible that these most recent kills are not by newbies? No one has the means to harness that much strength and speed. Only when a vampire is first turned does he/she have that kind of power, once they are prepped to control the urge this power weakens some." "He must have realized that the only way to truly be able to carry out his plan is to do it himself, but that doesn't explain how he has harnessed this new power of his. If we do not figure it out soon, it will certainly be the end of mankind as we know it." Katherine stated with gravity in her voice that sent everyone's heart falling to the floor. "How can this be...?" Deshali stated as he was rushing around the room to find a particular book. "I know I have heard of this before, in one of the books by the elders" he was talking more to himself than anyone in the room. "History has shown many people the error of their ways, but at a great cost. Here it is." Deshali was rushing through the pages of a rather large book. "Ahh, ok. Before a human is being turned, if it is done in such a way as to bring about irrational and overwhelming fear then on the moment, they are turned, their strength increases 10-fold. Of course the vampire must watch over his prey very carefully, as he only has mere seconds to drain them before the process is completed." "Ok, if that is the case this all makes sense," Katherine was dismayed at this new revelation. If Shariffi had indeed become so strong, how could they possibly fight him and win. Deshali was angered at this prospect. "All we have is the element of surprise. Everyone thinks that Shantini is the one who created all those newbies; no one knows they were just a distraction to give Shariffi more time. We have few choices here," Deshali continued, "There is a traitor amongst us. I have a few suspicions as to who it could be, but our primary target is Shariffi." Katherine knew that he was right; there was no way Shariffi could have known anything unless he had someone on the inside. "It looks like it is you and me, Katherine," Deshali stated with much sadness, for he knew they probably would not be coming back…

Chapter Fourteen

On the Move

"We need to stop for a bit. I am hungry and would like to get cleaned up," keep it together Ash. Random thoughts, I have less than a moment to form, plan and implement. "You okay?" Sarah questioned, looking puzzled at Ash. "Yeah, I just have a nervous stomach, that's all," okay, okay I can do this. What is the distance from the car to the bathroom? If 2 +2 =4, then 4+4 =8. I kept my thoughts random, trying not to focus on my plan. Unsure of how close a vampire would have to be to read my thoughts, I made sure that I did not stay focused on one thing for longer than a second.

My gut feelings about Sarah were not going away. A week into driving around aimlessly and I felt no safer than when we began our trip. Sarah's actions continued to seem too controlled. I was on high alert and I did not trust this woman. Just as I was about to flee, Harold stepped in front of me. "Come with me," Harold stated, looking grim. "What about Sarah?" Ashley questioned. How could they have known that I would try to run? What is Harold doing here? "I don't have time to explain right now, Ash. But I will as soon as we are away from here." Harold stated, rushing her towards a black beamer.

"Ok" was my only response. At least I would be away from Sarah, that was something. "Ash, I know you don't understand what is happening. I can't say that I fully understand myself, but this Sarah is not my Sarah." Harold stated with great remorse. "I don't know what they have done with her, or if she is still alive. I am just glad that we got to you before they could." A slight sigh of relief passed his lips as he climbed into the driver's seat. "I felt like something was not right. She did not seem like the woman that you described to me." I was more confused than before. But I was more relaxed now.

The satellite phone rang, I answered it without hesitation. "Hello." "Ashley, where are you?" Sarah stated angrily. "I am safe, no worries." I replied, looking at Harold who was intently looking at the road driving. "You know that your survival is dependent on me, how could you do this? Katherine will be furious." She screamed into the phone. "Harold will be taking care of me, for the rest of the trip." I relayed with much satisfaction. "Harold? He was here? But how?" Sarah's voice changed. "No worries then." Click the phone went dead.

"I knew it wouldn't be long before she called. I just hope that we have put enough distance between us to keep her from catching up." Harold stated[M2]. "Ok, so spill it! What is going on?" I demanded. "I am not sure if Katherine and Deshali made it out of their fight alive, because I almost didn't make it. All I know is that Katherine called me last night ordered me to get to you as fast as possible and get you as far away from Sarah as quickly possible. She said that Sarah was not my Sarah; that things had gone horribly wrong and I needed to make sure that you were safe." Harold stopped to take a deep breath. "That somehow they had gotten to Sarah and replaced her. This is where things get a little strange. Apparently, Sarah had an identical twin that was working with Shariffi. No one knew not even Sarah knew. She was changed at an older age than my Sarah, but being twins, they were similar enough that the difference wasn't noticeable at first. When she met up with us that night, she seemed off. I had no idea; I just thought she was worried about me. I chalked it up to the situation. Katherine found some type of evidence that proved that my Sarah was not the one with you. So needless to say here I am." Harold was trying very hard not to let his concern for his Sarah overwhelm him. "I am sorry that things have gotten so strange. I hope that your Sarah turns up soon and is okay." I did not know what else to say. "When will we be meeting up with Katherine?" I asked quietly. "When she calls and gives the all-clear." Harold was distracted, but his driving did not show it.

Chapter Fifteen

The Battle

Armed and dangerous, that was Deshali and Katherine, headed to Shariffi's place. What a chance they were taking going in alone, but they did not know who could be trusted. Shariffi has taken up residence in an old abandoned town that he had remolded to his specifications. Luckily, for Deshali, Ester knew who did the remodeling and was able to get plans that showed the changes. Ester was more than just Deshali's maid, she saw herself as his protector. She long ago sensed that something bad was coming and kept a low profile. She played up her disabilities to give her the edge she needed to get the information that she needed. Only Deshali, Katherine and Harold Knew that there was more to Ester than meets the eye. The plans showed a labyrinth of tunnels that connected under the town; some were shown to have been closed off. It was the closed-off tunnels that would be the element of surprise. There was no way that all the tunnels could be guarded, the most obvious ones for guards would be the ones that lead to direct access. Some of the markings were hard to read, two tunnels were not clearly marked on the plans, it was these that they would use to get in. On the original plans, the markings looked like closets, when in reality they were escape tunnels for slaves.

"Ok, I will take the south tunnel. You take the north

tunnel. We will meet in the middle and kill everyone we come across. If Shariffi stays true to his normal routine, he will be in the library. That is where we will meet and kill him." Deshali stated with no emotion.

"It is time to end this," Katherine agreed as they reached the tunnels. Good thing that vampires had such an excellent sight in the dark, otherwise how could they hope to surprise anyone? Slowly making their way down the tunnel, they noticed that the tunnel has a strange odor. It smelled like death. Although they did not see anything, they knew that death was ever-present, not just for the newbies and Shariffi, but for them as well. Katherine could not help but wonder if she would see her beloved again or was this the final ending. Katherine kept a mental image of Ashley in her mind, wanting to be with her and hold her. She knew that would not be possible until everyone was taken care of. She was not looking forward to this fight. So much was at stake. Katherine continued to walk behind Deshale until they finally came upon the fork in the tunnel. Placing a finger over his lips Deshali gestured to Katherine to continue down the tunnel. Slowly, step by step, her heart sank. Something is not right; she could feel it. Had they underestimated Shariffi? Would the two of them be able to bring him down?

A scream, more like a shriek echoes through the tunnel. Katherine is unable to tell how far way the scream was, but she knew she was getting close. Three newbies stood between Katherine and the entrance to the hotel. Katherine quickly and quietly killed the first of the three newbies. He did not know what hit him; the element of surprise was truly the only weapon Katherine had. As she removed the head of the newbie, the next one charged at her. "Guess the element of surprise is over now," Katherine thought to her-self. Hand to hand combat with this one. He was as strong as an ox, tall, and lanky. Every time he moved, he looked like he was dancing. Was I becoming soft in my old age? Katherine laughed to herself. The Newbie cut into Katherine's flesh as though it were a hot knife cutting through butter. One of the benefits of being a vampire, she didn't have to worry about bleeding to death. The cut was almost healed when the next wave of attack came, this time how-ever Katherine was ready. She pulled out her sword, swung it at the newbie and his head rolled onto the floor. Now it was time to finish the last one. He looked like a child, any hesitation could cost her, her life. Recovering quickly from the site of the child, Katherine swung and made con-tact with the newbies head. There was that scream again, only this time it was much closer, and Katherine could clearly tell where it was coming from. She rushed in the direction of the screams as there was something familiar about it. Another scream, only now Katherine was close enough to tell that someone else was talking in between the screams. Katherine could not tell who the person talk-ing was, but definitely knew the person screaming was Sarah. Slowly Katherine made her way towards the voices; it was surprising how deserted this area was. Where were the guards? Katherine should have been close enough now to have seen more guards, according to the plans, she should be just under the main house. Another scream this one sounded weak, surely Sarah could not endure much more.

Katherine came upon an opening; she could not have been more than a few feet from where they were. She slowly peeked around through the doorway. Sarah was strung up by her wrists to the ceiling; she had suffered a terrible beating or whipping from the look of it. Her abuser was just inches away with a sword ready to detach her head from her body. It was now or never, at least for Sarah's sake. Katherine charged into the room, in one fatal swoop, the abuser's head was rolling across the floor. With the next swing of her blade, she had released Sarah from her restraints catching her and laying her gently on the floor. Sarah turned her head towards Katherine, tears welling up in her eyes "you must hurry. It is a trap, a trap for Deshali." Katherine realizing what she was saying left her with a weapon and ran to save Deshali.

Deshali was gradually making his way through the tunnel, surprisingly, he did not run into any guards. Deshali had not lived so long by making foolish mistakes. He stopped and listened. It was too quiet. Looking at the plans he stood for a moment, the path that was laid out for him, according to it there have been at least two sets of guards for the section he was in now yet could not hear anything. He stood for a moment longer, his mind trying to put it together. Something was not right. He hears something, turns towards the sound and sees Katherine coming towards him in a blur. "It's a trap, I found Sarah being tortured down the other tunnel. She is on her way out. Looking at the map, I say we go this way" both of them looked at the map/plans again and agreed. Suddenly they both leap into action, moving very fast down a second tunnel. As they passed other tunnels, they could hear whispering. "Stay alert, they should be here any minute," someone was saying. Neither of them could make out who it was talking. They continued down the long tunnel, if they were correct in their choice they should be coming upon a door or gate, hard to tell which by the plans. There it was just a few feet in front of them. Katherine pulled Deshali by the arm and into a small alcove, "shhhh…" she had her finger over her lips. The sound of footsteps was clear, if they had not stopped, they would have missed hearing them, the sound was so light. They looked at each other puzzled. Were they being followed? If they were being followed, then by whom? Katherine thought to herself, "No matter, they will die as well."

Chapter Sixteen

Nowhere Land

Harold and I drove for hours in silence. I, trying very hard not to focus on any one thing for too long, but her mind kept going back to Katherine. How could this be happening? Please let her be okay, I was praying and begging. Suddenly, one of the tires blew out, the car fishtailed but Harold recovered quickly (he was an expert driver). "It's okay Ash, just a blowout," he stated trying to sound calm. I could tell that he was anything but calm. His grip on the steering wheel these last few miles had turned his knuckles white and caused indentions in the wheel. I only just realized that it had gotten dark; I was so deep in thought that I barely noticed the sun going down. "I will change the tire. You stay put in the car, Okay?" Harold did not sound so sure of himself. Ashley was starting to get a bad feeling about this sudden blowout. "Can I stretch my legs first and then get back in the car?" Ashley questioned. "Okay but make it fast. I do not want you out in the open too long. I am pretty sure we got far enough away from that woman, but I don't know if she had anyone else helping her that may have been trailing us," he stated with uncertainty in his voice. I only then just realized the enormous strain that he must be under, his love was also in trouble. "I am so sorry, Harold. I have been so worried about Katherine that I never realized how worried you must be about Sarah," I stated with agony. "It's okay, believe me, I understand. I was just thinking the same thing about you and your situation." Harold tried to smile. I went up to him and hugged him, "it will be alright, I know it will (I pray it will)." He hugged me back, and then suddenly I was on the ground behind him. "Ashley, RUN!!!" Harold was shouting at me. Run, where we are in the middle of nowhere? Scrambling to her feet she took off in the opposite direction of where Harold was looking. Suddenly she heard a loud thud, as though something or someone had been thrown into the side of the car. "There is nowhere for you to run out here," a voice said in her ear, and then everything went black....

Harold was fighting for his life. All the rage that he had been holding in for his missing Sarah burst at the seams. He was ripping and tearing with his bare hands. Never before had he been so savage. Katherine had taught him well how to control himself and the animal urges that could and would take over if you let them. All the years of holding it inside finally unleashed. The agony that he felt over the loss of his love (for he felt that surely she was dead) brought out a side of him that he did not know existed. After a few moments, he was standing there in the dark looking at the body parts of the vampires he had just killed and now lusted to kill again. On the wind, he smelled fear and charged in that direction, "oh, no. Not her. You will not be killing her tonight," Harold thought to himself as he went to save Ashley.

Chapter Seventeen

The Darkness

.... "Help!" I screamed at the top of my lungs. "Someone please help me!" I continued to yell despite knowing that no one was going to answer. There was only silence and darkness. I yelled and screamed until I no longer could. What was going to happen to me? This was scaring the hell out of me. No sounds. No wind blowing. No traffic noise. Nothing else: but silence and the musky smell of damp earth. It was so dark. Running my hand along the wall, I felt sticky wetness beneath my fingertips. My feet were soaked. Was the ground wet as well, was I standing in water?" I was alone in the dark; little did I know that it was the darkness of my mind that had me trapped. Make no mistake, my body was in mortal danger, but the immediate threat now came from my own mind. "Baby girl, what is the matter with you?" Granny spoke softly. "Granny, is that you? Where are you? I can hear you, but I can't see you?" I was confused. "It is me, child," Granny confirmed. "It is not your time, not yet child. Wake up! Wake up, NOW and run!" Granny's voice faded. I awoke with a start and did as I was told, not sure of where I was running to. Another loud thud like the one back at the car and the sound of someone gasping for air.... "Can't stop, must keep running," my mind was screaming.

Harold had caught up with them effortlessly. Looking at

them, he saw Ashley on the ground, was she dead? No, there was movement. The vampire was on the phone with someone, not paying attention. Another moment and Harold was on top of her. Taken by surprise, the breath was knocked out her. "What was that?" the false Sarah thought in a daze. "Not, that girl. There was no way she could be that strong," she tried to get to her feet but was unable to move, a stabbing pain in the middle of her chest. "My wife is probably dead because of you. But she will not have died in vain." Harold said with calmness in his voice. "I understand your loss, she was my twin and she was taken from me. But you are wrong, she is not dead. He promised me that she would not be killed." She whispered. "Then you are a bigger fool than I thought. He is not a man of his word, never was." Harold's hand was still in her chest, all he had to do was pull it out and she would be dead. "Wait, please. He is my maker; I had no choice. I understand now why he chose me. My sister is in the tunnels beneath his property; your friends are already there and will soon be dead. If you mean to save her you must hurry. Tell her I am sorry." With her last words, he tore his hand from her chest and with it came her heart, with his other hand his sword took off her head. He stood very still for a moment and just listened. Heavy breathing, from where? He listened harder and ran in the direction of the sound.

I kept running through the trees and shrubs, moving as fast as I could manage without losing my balance. "Keep going my child, you are almost there. Almost safe." Granny's voice softly leading her way. Thump. No air. I couldn't catch my breath. "It's okay Ashley, it's me Harold," his voice sounded like heaven and then she collapsed into his arms.

Chapter Eighteen

The Deceiver

Emory was standing with Shariffi in the middle of the library when Katherine and Deshali rushed the room. There was a chair closest to Shariffi with a high back, but you could still tell that it held someone in it. Katherine first thought was Ashley. She started towards the chair; Deshali held up his arm and stopped her. At that moment Shariffi turned the chair and there with her heart removed was his sister, Shantini. Deshali was taken aback, but only for a moment. Shariffi looked at him with disgust, "that is your weakness, people." "I have no such weakness. She was my sister, but that did not make her any less expendable." Shariffi stated devoid of emotion. You could tell he felt nothing. "That is not a weakness; it is the part of me that is still human," Deshali spoke quietly, but clearly.

"Your sister was willing to die for you." Deshali was slowly moving into a better position from which to strike. "And so, she did. Now the two of you will be joining her." Before he finished his sentence, he dove towards Deshali, who moved mere seconds before contact could be made. "You should have learned years ago, never underestimate your opponent," Deshali stated allowing a small smirk to shape his lips. "I am not the old man you think is so easily beaten. I have not lived for over a thousand years without possessing my own special abilities," with that he moved in for the kill. But Shariffi has anticipated his move and countered it very skillfully. Emory was trying to escape the room when Katherine removed his head. "You should have stuck to being neutral at least you would have kept your head that way." Katherine was finishing up Emory when the guards started to arrive, one at first then another and another. However by this time Sarah was back to herself, well as much as she could be considering the torture she went through. It was apparent that if she was to live, they had meant to leave her disfigured. It would not matter to Harold, what her appearance looked like; it was her heart and soul that he cared about. She fought with great courage as she took down two of the guards in one swipe of her sword. Katherine was at her back and they fought back to back.

Deshali and Shariffi were at a standoff. Shariffi trying to use words to throw him off. "The betrayal in your counsel goes far deeper than just Emory. Whether I lose or win today makes no difference, there will be change. I will not be held back any longer nor will the others. We are tired of not taking our rightful place; above the cattle we call humans. I too am human, but a better version." Shariffi was ranting, for he knew that he was losing. Deshali looked at him for a long moment and then spoke, "what you say may be true, but I will spend every day of my life making sure that does not happen," then lunging towards him with his entire mite, but in a second he was gone. "What the hell?" Deshali yelled out confused. "Katherine, he is gone." "Through the wall, there is another tunnel," Katherine yelled as he began running towards Deshali. The bookcase gave way to a tunnel and they ran through.

At the other end, Shariffi was met by a surprise. I and Harold were rushing through the tunnel, going more by instinct than knowledge. Left, right, right then left, surely, they were lost down here. Harold said, keep to the right, but Granny's voice said "No, child it is time for what you were born to do. Now to the left," She commanded. Ashley broke away from Harold and ran to the left with the dagger that Katherine had given her in front. Running as if the devil were behind her, little did she know that the devil would soon be in front of her. All at once, she felt like she had hit a wall, but it could not have been a wall for it was softer than a wall. She hit and fell to the ground. Suddenly there was light, it was Harold behind her. They both were staring ahead, it was Shariffi. "Not you! You are supposed to be dead! This is not possible. I have kept you at bay for decades, I have killed you more times than anyone should be allowed to die and yet you come back again and again to torture me," Shariffi stopped to draw in a breath that did not exist for him, for as he opened his mouth to speak his head hit the floor and his body soon followed. Katherine came to me, I was dazed and confused trying to make sense of what I was just told. Decades? Me? "You have done well, my child. Now enjoy the rest of your life. Your destiny has been fulfilled at last. I love you...." Granny's voice faded away into the darkness.

"I was so worried about you. I thought for sure they had found you and ...." Katherine's voice trailed off; she could not bring herself to speak the words. "I too thought the same of you, my love" I tightened my arms around her not wanting to let go. "Harold, Harold you there baby?" Sarah's voice was pleading. You could hear the fear in her voice afraid she had lost her beloved husband of 55 years. "Woman, you should know by now that you won't be getting rid of me that easy," he smiled and scooped her up in his arms, "Well at least not for another 55 years I should think." They were smiling as their heads came together for a kiss.

Deshali was relieved but sad at the same time. He had lost some close friends tonight and over the next few weeks he would surely lose more, but for now, he would relish the moment.

Acknowledgement

Thank you for the front cover:
Illustration done by: Fiverr.com/mahinoor888

About The Author

Tara Moats

Tara Moats is a new author. This is her first offical book. She has plans to make this book a series.